my sicilian promise

TESS RINI

ISBN: 979-8-9904586-1-1 (e-book)

ISBN: 979-8-9904586-2-8 (paperback)

Tessrini.com

Publisher: One Punch Productions, LLC

Cover design and interior formatting by *Hannah Linder Designs*

RINALDI FAMILY

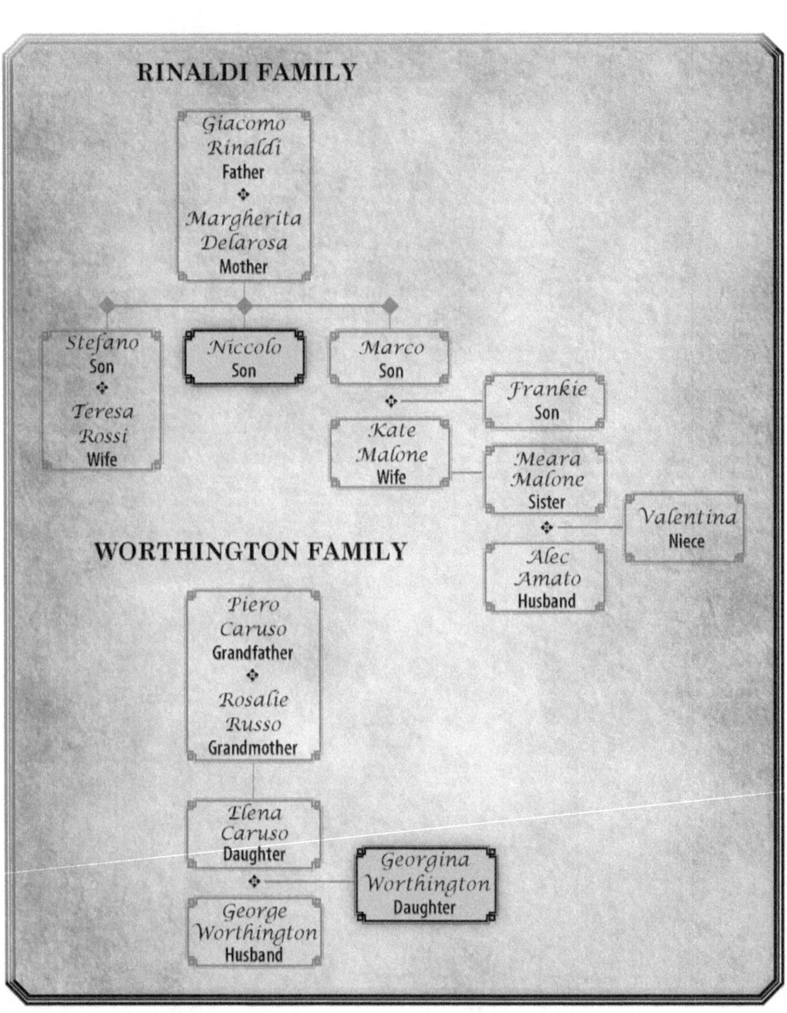

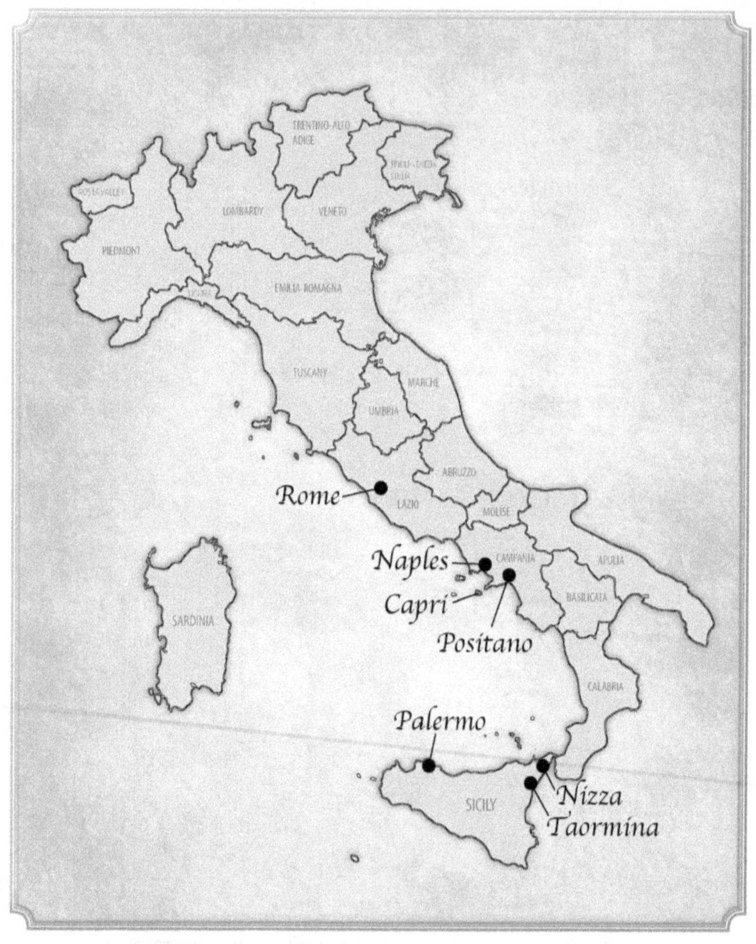

Where we travel in *My Sicilian Promise* (with Rome as a reference!)

one

Niccolo Rinaldi touched the brim of his black baseball hat, pulling it tighter down over his forehead. He shrugged the lapels of his jacket over his shoulders. Never mind that it was a bright sunny spring day, he wore the dark leather jacket to give himself a shield of sorts. He ran a hand across his tired eyes and tried not to think about his churning stomach. He couldn't leave his post now after waiting several hours. It was almost time. Glancing at his watch for what must be the tenth time in ten minutes, he impatiently frowned. Where was she?

As if the universe were answering him, a vintage white Bentley purred to a stop in front of St. Paul's Cathedral. Niccolo stepped back guardedly. The newsstand proprietor glared at him, rolling his eyes. He had asked Niccolo several times if there was something he could help him with, but Niccolo had only shaken his head absentmindedly. No one could help him. At this point, that was the only thing he was certain of.

His heart pounded as the chauffeur stepped out of the vehicle to open the door nearest to the cathedral. Across the street, a mass of white emerged from the elegant car. The bride's hands smoothed out the billowing folds and ruffles of the wedding gown that seemed to envelop her slight frame. Standing tall, she resembled a figurine atop a wedding cake. Bridesmaids came running down the stairs to greet her. She pushed back the veil impatiently, which was held in place by a shining tiara. Her beautiful blonde hair was regretfully pulled back severely into a complicated knot behind her head.

Climbing the stairs carefully, she suddenly stopped and slowly turned her head and upper torso. Her gaze swept across the street, almost as if she sensed his presence. By now, he was within the safe confines of the newsstand. Even if she saw his silhouette, there was no way she would suspect it was him. From this distance, he regretted he couldn't see her spectacular eyes— a rich blue that darkened when she was excited or angry. He could never forget that color.

Frowning slightly, she turned back around, bending to listen intently to a flower girl who appeared at her side. Lifting her skirts, she began to climb the stairs again, her back straight with determination, the enormous train of her gown trailing behind her regally.

An older gentleman also emerged from the car, and Nico frowned as the man placed his top hat on his head determinedly and followed his daughter. Never had Nico felt such loathing for a human being. Hatred was usually not in his character, but the darkness washed over him. It seared his soul, and if Nico wasn't already in such pain, he would have tried to find a way to hate the man more.

Photographers were now racing up the stairs to get photos of the gorgeous bride. The cathedral's bells were pealing across the London sky as if the most fabulous event was occurring. Only for Nico, it was the worst day of his life. The only woman he had ever truly loved was about to marry another man.

"Are you going to buy anything or not?"

The newsstand operator was clearly frustrated with him.

Digging into his pocket, Nico pulled out a large bill and handed it to him.

"My apologies. Thank you for allowing me to occupy your stand," Nico said formally. Glancing one more time at the cathedral, he walked slowly away.

The man shouted after him, "Hey, for this, you can stand here all day, mate!"

Nico ignored the vendor's offer. There was nothing left to see. Georgina would be someone else's wife by the time he got back to his hotel.

～

TWO MONTHS LATER

"How's one of my favorite brothers-in-law?"

Nico turned in his chair as the beautiful brunette sat next to him. Her wide grin wasn't the only evidence of her happiness. She practically glowed. And why not? She was happily married to Nico's brother, Marco, and they were ecstatic new parents to a baby son, Frankie.

"Just wonderful," Nico answered dryly.

Kate gave him a joking frown. "You look just wonderful," she responded sarcastically. She elbowed him teasingly. "What gives? Why so glum, chum?"

He rolled his eyes at her teasing. "I just don't like weddings," he explained through gritted teeth.

"Uh, sorry, *mio fratello*, but I saw you dancing the night away at the last few weddings—not only mine but also your brother and cousin's. So, it seems as if only this wedding seems to be a drag. Aren't you happy for my sister and her new husband?" she asked mockingly.

Nico glanced over at the crowded dance floor. Kate's sister,

Meara and her husband Alec were dancing as if they were the only two people in the room. Meara, a tall, stunning redhead, was a force of nature and known internationally for her leadership in the tech world. She had left that behind and now was the executive director of the foundation Marco had started on behalf of the Rinaldi Family. Alec, who coincidentally was Kate's doctor during her pregnancy, was on the board of the foundation. The two had met as Meara took over the reins, but apparently, there had been some bumps along the way. Alec was a single father to his niece following the death of his sister. Meara, who never imagined herself being a mother, had needed time to adjust to the idea. From the looks of them throughout the day, the couple was deeply in love, and Meara had grown into being a doting mother to young Valentina.

Watching the couple so immersed in each other made his entire body ache, but now was not the time to show it. Instead, he leaned over and kissed Kate's cheek. "Of course, I'm happy for Meara and Alec, *mia sorella*. I know the whole family is celebrating. Please don't let my bad mood ruin the evening."

Concern registered on her face. "Nico, I don't think I've ever seen you in a bad mood. I'm a great listener if you want to talk."

He sighed. "It's a long story."

She put her chin on her folded hands. "Isn't that interesting? I've got loads of time." To prove it, she kicked off her shoes and picked up a bottle of wine that sat on the table. Pouring herself a glass, she topped off his. "Spill it. Tell me everything."

Nico glanced around nervously. "My brothers don't even know the entire story. And it's a long one. Marco is going to miss you shortly and be stalking over here to claim you for the next dance."

Kate glanced around and shrugged. "He's in deep conversation with some of the company's board members. And he can wait. This is important."

Nico shook his head sadly.

"It's a woman, isn't it?" asked Kate softly. At his slight nod, she smiled a little. "I knew it. I bet Meara...well never mind that now."

"Meara knows?" Nico's eyes grew wide.

Kate smiled. "She was the first one to notice your... demeanor. She was on her way over here when her groom pulled her onto the dance floor. You're lucky she dispatched me instead. Meara would have already cracked you like an egg by now, shining a bright light in your eyes." Kate chuckled. "When we were kids, she could get anything out of me. I never stood a chance."

Nico grinned for a minute, leaning back in his chair. He had loosened his navy tie and slung his jacket over his chair. His black wavy hair was probably all disheveled from running his hands through it. Kate often told him he resembled his handsome brother, Marco. Marco was so striking he looked like he should be on the cover of a men's fashion magazine, and Nico didn't see any similarities. He glanced over at his other brother, Stefano, who was dancing with his wife, Teresa. Stefano's face had a lean, chiseled appearance, with a prominent jawline. Other than dark hair, Nico didn't resemble him at all.

Kate's voice broke into his thoughts. "What's her name?"

"George," Nico answered automatically. At Kate's quizzical look, he smiled a little. "Georgina. But I always called her George or Georgie."

"Are you in love with her?"

He shook his head. "It doesn't matter. She's married."

"You fell in love with a married woman?" Kate asked incredulously.

"No!" Nico responded loudly. Glancing around, he lowered his voice. "I fell in love with her when she was single. Two months ago, she got married."

Kate nodded understandingly. "Well, that explains your mood, I guess. Did you have a chance to tell her how you felt before...uh, the big day?"

Nico shook his head. "It's a long story," he repeated. "Maybe someday I'll tell you, but for now, it's not worth repeating." Standing abruptly, he held out his hand. "May I have this dance, *mia sorella*?"

Kate stood slowly, shaking out the folds of her gown. "You're trying to distract me. You Rinaldi brothers are famous for it. But just know that I'll be circling back at some point." She arched an eyebrow. "And I'm not putting my shoes back on."

He grinned and swung her out on to the dance floor. Pulling back, he smiled at her. "And I thought I was your favorite *fratello*? Forget Stiff Stefano. I'm much more fun and you know it!"

Kate's musical laugh rang out and for a moment, his heart felt lighter.

two

TWO YEARS LATER

Nico drove through the tranquil seaside town of Nizza di Sicilia, past the colorful pastel-colored houses and through the town center with its family-run restaurants and small piazzas. His Jeep easily began to climb the hill, traveling by the rows and rows of lemon trees that stretched as far as he could see. His black hair ruffled as the wind blew through the windows. He breathed deeply, inhaling the sweet scent of the spring day in the small but beautiful coastal Italian *comune*. Earlier that morning, Nico had flown into Palermo, about 180 kilometers to the east, and driven straight to Nizza.

It felt exhilarating to be back. The island of Sicily had captured his heart as a young man when his *Zio* Angelo had sent him there to work summers in the lemon and olive groves. Nico had run in these very hills as a boy, tending to the soil and doing odd jobs for the farmers on his uncle's land and neighboring farms. There was something about Sicily that grounded him and made him feel an inner peace. He hadn't felt that way for a long time.

The last two years had gone by quickly, and Nico made the most of it. Though his quest for higher education started several months prior to Alec and Meara's wedding, Nico had committed even more strongly to it, taking eighteen more months to gain certifications and degrees in advanced agriculture at a university in Northern California. As a Vice President for Oro Industries, he pleaded with Marco to allow him time off to explore his passion in agriculture and sustainable farming. Marco had shaken his head with a bemused expression, but he said he understood Nico's desire. Nico grew up working with the soil, and though he accepted responsibility for the operations of Oro Industries' vast number of lemon and olive groves, it never fulfilled him. Despite his long days, he still spent any free time working in his greenhouses or his plot of land that his mother had given him at the family's estate on their first lemon grove.

What was it that drew him to Sicily? It was true he was half Sicilian—his father's side. Grimacing slightly as his father's shadow entered his mind, he shook off the imminent bad mood that often followed the memories of his early childhood. His father had abandoned his mother with three young sons. Nico, being the youngest, had only fleeting recollections of Giacomo Rinaldi. Often, he wondered if the remembrances were even real or something his conscious conjured up after seeing the family's old photos. His mother had made peace with her husband on his deathbed. Marco, once the most bitter of the three brothers, had also come to some sort of acceptance. Stefano was still trying to get to a more positive place, and Nico was forced to admit he still struggled. Their mother once surmised that it was because Nico felt a kinship with his father, who also believed the soil was at the heart of their lives. Was he similar to his father? He grimly hoped only the best parts of his father's DNA translated to him.

Nico grew up watching the weather patterns in their part of the world slowly change. The floods became fiercer and more frequent, the sun more blistering, and other environmental impacts threatened their land. His interest in the changes in climate and his introduction to regenerative farming early on made him now a leader in the innovative field. Discovering that thousands of years of conventional farming was destroying the soil, Nico emphasized to others it was time to relearn how to do things to give their soil the life it needed. For the soil also was imperative for humans to survive. His education had only enhanced his knowledge, as he found he already knew the techniques they must embrace in what he called a farming evolution. Appearing at several international symposiums, his expertise was now recognized. Not a conceited man, Nico also believed his accolades came from his position and the acclaim of his family's dynasty. Oro Industries had made a name for itself and now with his brother, who took over for *Zio* Angelo upon his death, was recharting its course. Marco, a charming and captivating CEO, was often in the headlines. And his brilliant idea of creating the Angelo Foundation, a charitable organization that aimed to improve health care access for those in need in his homeland, was truly remarkable.

So much landed on Marco's shoulders, and though it wasn't necessarily fair, his oldest brother seemed to accept his role. Now Stefano was also transitioning his own responsibilities so he could carve out a niche pasta company. In addition, Stefano had recently hosted a popular television show about Italian cuisine as a favor for their cousin Lucca, a renowned actor who had left Hollywood for a life in Italy. He wanted to create content that reflected his love of his homeland while also carving out a new path for him and his new wife, Ellie. She was a brilliant painter and was thrilled at the idea of a simpler life, having grown up in the spotlight with her own parents who were famous actors.

Nico was happy for Marco when he finally found Kate, who had literally fallen into his arms after hurting her ankle in Positano. Then came Lucca, who fell in love with Ellie, who coincidentally was decorating the cake for Marco and Kate's wedding.

Stefano was next. He fell madly in love with Teresa, Kate's best friend. A former television producer, Teresa had transformed the often-serious Stefano into a personable and likeable host on Lucca's show. The series won acclaim and fans now were demanding a second season as they embraced Stefano's passion for Italian cuisine.

Kate's observation about Nico dancing with joy at each wedding was correct. He was thrilled for both his brothers and cousin. He had long pushed his own true love down, focusing instead on his passion for the land.

After winding through the hills, he finally pulled off the road, and set the brake on his Jeep. He stared at his favorite property in Sicily: A Fifteenth Century lemon grove stood before him, sloping downward in silent splendor. Its trees were drooping slightly with green lemons that would eventually ripen into bright yellow fruit. Bees happily buzzed around white blossoms on the trees. The grove still had an ancient stone irrigation system that wound through the grove, and was still used to hydrate the trees. He slowly got out of the vehicle, taking his sunglasses off. Frowning, he fingered the trees' leaves and slid his hand down to their bark. Taking a small knife out of his pocket, he used it to peel some bark and then smelled it. Bending over, he ran the soil between his fingers and inhaled the smell as well.

Standing, Nico walked slowly through the grove, listening to the wind rustle through the faded green leaves. Though he would have liked to have delved into the soil more to explore its health, he was dressed nicer than usual in his cream-colored chinos and dark brown shirt. Receiving an urgent message from an old friend who was a solicitor, Nico traveled to Nizza immediately. He wasn't sure why he was summoned, and the solicitor was remarkably tight-lipped.

Glancing over at a stone bench, he wandered over to stroke

its warmth in the scorching sun. The breeze ruffled his hair, and he brushed it impatiently from his eyes.

"We used to sit for hours on this bench, talking and dreaming."

Nico's hand froze. His heart pounded, and a cold shock ran through his body. Taking a deep breath, he turned toward the voice. He acknowledged the ravishing blonde with a cool, slight nod. "*Ciao*, Georgina."

GEORGINA WORTHINGTON BLINKED to reassure herself the stunningly attractive man before her was truly real. Nico's face frequently played a starring role in her dreams. When she closed her eyes at night, the image of Nico's laughing eyes, framed by the longest eyelashes she had ever seen on a man, filled her mind. Each morning, a bittersweet feeling washed over her as she woke, realizing that it was all just a dream. Though he was completely nonexistent in any aspect of her life, she could never shake his presence in her subconscious. Since their fateful encounter at sixteen years old, he had become a permanent fixture in the recesses of her heart, a steady ache that never ceased.

Tossing her blonde wavy hair behind her shoulder, she brushed her suddenly sweaty palms down her top to her jeans. She had chosen to wear a simple blue-and-white striped blouse tucked into a pair of worn jeans, to avoid appearing as if she dressed up for him. Only she had because what seemed like a lifetime ago, Nico once said she looked amazing in jeans. He didn't have to know she'd held onto that piece of information, and it was doubtful he remembered his casual comment from years ago. If his current icy stare were any indication, it was unlikely he would even notice what she was wearing.

A grown-up Nico was now standing before her. Except one

thing was different. Her Nico, the one that figured in her thoughts and dreams, always had a ready grin, framed by deep dimples. Hardly welcoming, his demeanor now was stiff and wary. He hadn't even come forward to give her a kiss on each cheek, as Italian custom dictated. She swallowed with difficulty.

"*Ciao,* Nico," she responded softly, surprised at how hoarse her voice sounded. Her throat was dry. She swallowed again. "It's lovely to see you again."

His frown grew fiercer, if that were possible. What was wrong with him? Even when she used to infuriate him, he had never looked at her so venomously. Although their relationship disintegrated, it was years ago. His appearance now was undeniably intimidating.

"I wish I could agree with you," he said coldly. "What are you doing here, Georgina?"

She frowned a little. "You used to call me George."

"That was when we were...friends."

She looked away from his dark gaze, trying not to show what a blow he had dealt her. Despite the absence of any communication, she clung to the belief that they were friends, even if it existed solely in her own thoughts. Over the years, she even erroneously assumed that if she ever truly needed him, all she had to do was reach out and he would come to her. Apparently, that had been a fantasy of her own making.

She remembered their first encounter as if it was yesterday. She had been picking lemons at this very grove. Her grandmother sent her to gather the ripe fruit, enough to fill a basket for the family's use. A truck suddenly roared up, stopping near the grove. A group of teenage boys, who she assumed were workers in her grandfather's fields, jumped easily out of the truck bed. Loud and obnoxious, they entered the grove, dragging their tools behind them. Shy by nature, Georgie quickly retreated to a corner. But in her rush to escape, she dropped her basket of lemons and tripped over her own two feet, landing face first in the grass. She heard shouts of mocking laughter from the boys, but Nico ran to her, instantly offering her a helping hand. He then knelt and joined her in picking up the lemons, placing them into her basket. She glanced up into his black eyes and her heart did a somersault like never before. Georgie instantly knew her life would never be the same. As they stood, life simply halted. The moment was broken by the boys who demanded to know her name. When she told them quietly, enunciating Georgina with her proper British accent, they chortled and called her King George. Except Nico. He slowly grinned at her with a warmth that she only felt from the sun. It melted her insides, and she almost glowed. Abruptly, he was pulled away by his friends, but the moment became permanently ingrained in her mind.

"Buongiorno!"

Georgie's thoughts were interrupted as she turned to see her grandfather's solicitor, Luciano, who had called this meeting. Walking determinedly toward them, he greeted them enthusiastically in Italian. The older gentleman with graying hair was tanned from Sicily's powerful sun. He wore a long-sleeved dress shirt with a small scarf at his neck and khaki pants. He carried a briefcase, ready to do business.

Georgie interrupted him, after being greeted by his brief hug and kisses. "Luciano, do you mind if we speak English? My Italian is a bit rusty."

She didn't turn her head, but Nico was probably smirking. In the old days, he would have teased her about her Italian, prodding her to keep trying, working on her accent, and laughing at her chaotic sentences.

"*Si, si,*" Luciano agreed. Glancing around, he indicated the trees before them with a wave of his hand. "I asked to meet here because I wanted Nico to see the current state of the original lemon grove."

Nico greeted the older man respectfully before grimacing.

"What happened, Luciano? It's painfully neglected," he said with disgust. "Georgina, I thought *Nonno* employed better managers than this. I'll have to speak to him about it."

Georgie couldn't help the tears that formed in her eyes. "Oh, Nico," she finally choked out.

"He wouldn't even have to deal with this if he wasn't so stubborn! I told him I would take care of it. There is so much that needs to be done! I have offered repeatedly to buy this land from him! He just keeps telling me to wait." He waved his arm toward the trees. "This is disgraceful. And if this grove looks this bad, I can't imagine what his other hectares look like. Maybe we should go up to the farm and find out. Then I'm going to sit down with him and demand he sell it all to me."

"Nico," Georgie tried again. She swallowed the gigantic lump in her throat.

"That stubborn old man! It's not right!" he bellowed again.

"Nico, *Nonno* is dead!" she shouted. Clapping a hand over her mouth, her eyes grew wide. She had meant to tell him in a gentler manner, knowing how much Nico loved her grandfather. Now she couldn't keep the tears from falling freely.

Nico looked at her incredulously. "That's not true! I talked with him almost a week ago! He sounded strong."

Georgie turned so her back was to Nico. She couldn't take his anger anymore, and she impatiently brushed the tears from her cheeks. It was too difficult to remain composed and calm.

Luciano looked at the couple uncomfortably. "Georgina's grandfather and my dear friend Piero had cancer. It spread quickly, and he refused any further treatment."

"Did you know?" Nico asked quietly.

Calmer now, she turned around and fixed her gaze on him. "He didn't tell me anything. When I was last here, he seemed fine, though he was a bit thin. I thought that was because he was missing *Nonna* and not eating properly."

He frowned. "When was that?"

"Two months ago."

Nico turned his head away from her, and there were likely tears in his eyes. "I hadn't seen him for quite a while," he said huskily. "I was in the states and then traveling. I tried to call him as often as possible. He never said a word about being sick."

No one spoke. The hill was eerily silent, with only the faint rustling of the wind whispering through the lemon trees.

"He's already been buried with just me, Mum and Luciano there," Georgie finally said. "That was his wish. Of course, he wanted to be buried right next to my grandmother. He told me once that *Nonna*'s large funeral nearly broke him, and the thought of putting me or Mum through that was something he couldn't bear to think about."

"Your mother is here, too?"

Georgie nodded. "We came for the burial, but she went back to Palermo. She's going to stay there with friends until the *festa*."

Nico looked confused. "*Festa*? You're hosting a party?"

"Luciano tells me it's what he wanted. One big last party," Georgie answered, smiling sadly.

Nico stared at her silently. He finally walked a few yards away with slumped shoulders. After a minute, Luciano cleared his throat.

"Er, yes, well, we are here today to discuss the terms of Piero's will. Why don't we go up to Maria's restaurant and talk? I asked you to meet here so you could see the original grove. Later, if you want, we can continue up the hill and you can also tour the rest of the farm."

Georgie looked quizzically at Luciano and then at Nico's slouched back. "Why would Nico need to do that? I thought you asked him here today because *Nonno* left him something."

Luciano looked uncomfortable. "I'd prefer we discuss this over lunch."

"I'm not hungry," Nico and Georgie said at the same time.

Nico turned around, and they glanced quickly at each other

before averting their gazes. She turned to look at Luciano, taking pity on the older gentleman. "Let's go up the hill to *Nonno's* house, and I'll make something if we want to eat."

"You only know how to make pancakes," Nico responded flatly.

Georgie gave him a level stare. "Nico, it's been a long time since you've seen me. People *can* change."

"Oh, you've changed," he remarked dryly.

She turned slightly away from him, and he stepped toward her. "Georgie, I'm sorry." He took a deep breath. "Listen, it's been a long time since you or I saw each other. And we both know that didn't end well. But let's put that aside for now. This isn't the time. This has been a tremendous shock, and we're both grieving. Let's go to *Nonno's* house and hear what Luciano has to say."

She hesitated but then nodded in agreement. As they walked through the lemon grove, she lovingly stroked some leaves as she walked through the rows of trees. Just standing in the grove—neglected or not—gave her a connection to *Nonno*. This grove, the smallest of all Nonno's hectares, was where he was the happiest. It had been handed down through the family for six centuries. It meant everything to him. The wind whipped through her hair, and she heard the whisper as it swept through the trees. Taking a deep breath, she smelled the tangy citrus that lingered in the air no matter what season it was. It brought her back to a simple time, where the trees were abundant and thriving with fruit. Perhaps its timelessness was what her grandfather had loved. It must have transported him back to his own youth where he worked alongside his own grandfather in this very soil.

She swallowed the lump in her throat. It was also where she had met the love of her life.

three

Georgie put the tall glasses of lemonade and some biscuits she had bought at the local *pasticceria* on the table and sat down on the veranda of her grandparents' house. It sat high on the hill, just a kilometer from the original lemon grove. The house was large by Sicilian standards and painted beige to blend with the landscape. It overlooked the hectares of lemon trees that stood proudly in perfect formation below them.

Clearing his throat, Luciano opened his briefcase and put on his glasses. Nico, who had been leaning on a pillar looking out at the farm below them, walked over, pulled up a chair, and sat down. He nodded his thanks politely and took a long sip. For the first time, he smiled a little.

"*Nonno*'s lemons taste better than any others," he remarked. "There's just something about them."

Georgie gave a wobbly smile. "He thought they were the best, too. He was so proud of his land," she said with a muffled snob. She sniffed. "Sorry. It's just coming over me in waves."

Nico quickly averted his gaze. She saw how hard he swallowed and knew he was still in shock. She turned to stare at the farm below, stretching as far as her eyes could see.

Luciano cleared his throat and glanced at them above his glasses. "Are we ready?" Without waiting for their response, he began reading. The first part of the will focused on wishes for no funeral and outlined details for a *festa* instead, including food and the guest list. It was to be a party held at the original lemon grove. There was an area behind the shed where there was a large grassy area with no crops.

The next few paragraphs were the disposal of some of his belongings. He left odds and ends from his estate to various friends and neighbors. To Luciano, he left some of his woodworking machinery.

"My grandson has become quite skilled," Luciano remarked, looking at them above the paperwork. Georgie smiled a little. "That's nice. *Nonno* owned a lot of useful equipment. He even made that rocking chair over there. It was for Nonna, and after she passed, that's where he always sat." Turning, she stared at his empty wooden rocking chair gliding with the wind. The hours spent sitting with him on the veranda always filled her with happiness.

Luciano put down the papers and took off his glasses. "The house of course, is yours, Georgie. If you don't want it, he suggests selling it to someone local. He was most firm about that."

She nodded and looked away, back down to the trees. "And the farm," she added.

Luciano cleared his throat. "Well, as to that. Not quite. All of his property belongs to both you and Nico, and his wishes are that Nico oversees the management of it."

Georgie stood abruptly. "That can't be true. He always told me the land was mine."

"Well, it is," Luciano said soothingly. "Half yours, of course. If either of you choose to sell it, the other one has the first right of refusal."

"What if I don't want Nico to manage it? I mean, *Nonno* had people for years who managed it."

"Sadly, as you saw from the original lemon grove, it has not been taken care of as it should be," Luciano told her gently. "The people your *Nonno* leaned on over the years have grown older. Their children and grandchildren have moved away from Nizza to bigger cities."

"As I said earlier, we discussed me taking over the management for some time," Nico said. "Things have changed. Farming is evolving, and the old methods your grandfather used are no longer working to preserve the land. He knew all this, and I told him repeatedly I would take care of it. The last time we talked, he refused, but for the first time, he told me to wait a month. Now I know why."

Georgie stared at him, blinking back the tears. "I guess he knew I didn't have the knowledge to take care of the farm. I understand that. But I can't believe he gave you half of it."

Nico shook his head sadly. "You never understood our relationship, did you? I thought of Piero as my grandfather, too. He was always there for me. I wish I could have been here this last month."

"Me, too," Georgie said softly.

"Too busy jetting around the world?" Nico asked dryly.

Georgie looked confused. "*Nonno* told you? He promised not to."

"About what? I just assume you are living the high life. You know the life your father always wanted for you."

She glanced up at his sarcastic tone. He was so unlike the Nico she remembered. Opening her mouth, she quickly shut it again. She wasn't up to fighting with him.

Luciano looked from one to the other. "Yes, well, I'll let you two, uh, catch up." He stood swiftly, stuffing his papers into his briefcase. "You will both get a copy of the will. My office will send it soon. I assume I'll see you both at the *festa*. Let me know when it is to be, Georgie."

"Of course, Luciano," she said, standing and walking around the table to kiss his weathered cheek. "Thank you for being such a good friend to *Nonno*."

Nico stood as well, and he grimly put an arm on the man's shoulder. He departed, getting in the car with a single wave. His sedan glided down the hill around the farm and disappeared around a corner.

Nico turned and eyed her mockingly. "And now we'll catch up."

NICO STRUGGLED to keep his expression serious as Georgie came out to the veranda, balancing a giant plate of pancakes, a bottle of maple syrup under her arm. It was a lost cause; he couldn't keep his lips from twitching.

"Go ahead and laugh. I make bloody good pancakes!"

"I know you do. *Grazie*. I admit I am hungry now," Nico said, standing to take the platter from her and placing it on the table. He took a deep breath. "Hmmm, lemon ricotta?"

"Is there any other kind?" she asked, placing the bottle of syrup on the table. Reaching into the pocket of her apron, she took out a shaker of powdered sugar and added it to the table. Quickly casting the apron aside, she said, "I'm sorry there wasn't much else in *Nonno*'s house. I only did a quick shop last night."

He took a sip of the lemonade she had refreshed earlier. Sitting there with her, he could feel his mind spinning, trying to make sense of the surreal moment. The thought of asking about her life now was agonizing, but he had to. It would hopefully persuade his heart to move on. It wasn't fair to push her when she was grieving, but he needed answers. But first, they should take a few minutes to just get used to each other again. He started with a safe topic.

"You've been in Palermo with your mother?"

She nodded, clearly savoring the fluffy pancake in her mouth before swallowing and finally offering a response. "We were staying at a hotel, but then she went to visit friends for a few days. I think it will be good for her."

"What about you? Are you staying here?" Nico asked, spearing a pancake and placing it on his plate.

"I'm going to stay here until the *festa.* I don't know after that," she said uncertainly. "This is all so...sudden."

Nico took a bite and almost moaned. He had to admit, she did make darn good pancakes. He smiled a little as a wave of nostalgia ran over him. It was the only thing she had ever known how to cook. As a teenager, he often dined with Georgie's grandparents. But even after demolishing *Nonna's* delicious cooking, his teenage appetite would often leave him hungry later into the night. Frequently, Georgie whipped up pancakes for him after they crept back to the kitchen. Nostalgia flooded his heart as he remembered the late nights, the stolen bites, and the secret kisses they shared, always anxious Georgie's grandparents might catch them. Fortunately, they slept soundly.

It had taken some time for them to get to that romantic phase. The first summer after their quick meeting, he was kept busy working. Often, he tried to get a glimpse of *Nonno's* blonde British granddaughter, but it was challenging. When he did, it was unfortunate that he was surrounded by other teenage boys who whistled and shouted teasing remarks. He had been equally ridiculous, playfully joining in on the King George jokes, all while observing her as she effortlessly completed simple chores at the house near the farm. When he was caught staring, *Nonna* shooed him away with a dish towel, muttering about *stupido ragazzi.*

The next summer was different. Older now, he finally came to the realization the girls in his class were rather fascinating. Though he had one or two crushes and a few kisses along the way, a blonde curly-haired girl remained in the recesses of his mind.

Playing it cool that summer, Nico demonstrated to the foreman he was more mature than the others. This ultimately earned him respect and better assignments. Soon, he began working more closely with *Nonno* himself. Piero was a strongly built, stout Sicilian man who believed deeply in his commitment to the land. It struck a deep chord with Nico, and soon he forgot he was trying to impress the older man so he could get closer to his granddaughter. Instead, he soaked up Piero's knowledge and passion for the soil. It wasn't until he had been working at the man's side for a while that he received a dinner invitation.

That first night, Nico was tongue-tied and nervous. Georgie spoke with such proper English. Her grandparents were committed to teaching her Italian but encouraged her to speak English around Nico so he could improve his own skills. He couldn't tear his eyes away as he watched her carefully arranging the platters of mouthwatering homemade Italian cuisine on the table. It wasn't until their second or third dinner that they were given permission to enjoy a stroll on the veranda. They eventually sat on the steps overlooking the farm and talked for hours. Nico told her funny little jokes that she accused him of making up. Other nights, they were allowed to take walks, often finding a patch of grass where they could lie gazing at the stars. It was obvious from the beginning that Georgie was very shy. Despite her impeccable manners, he could tell that she had never been alone with a boy before. Drawing her out took considerable time, slowly building her confidence until she finally came to trust him. As they laid there, he found his hand slowly moving toward hers, until just their pinky fingers intertwined. The warmth of her hand made his heart race.

One Sunday, when there was no work or chores, they sat on the stone bench in the original lemon grove. They arched their necks, watching as the sun dipped behind fluffy clouds in the vibrant blue sky.

"Did you ever wonder what it would be like to fly?" Georgie asked suddenly.

Nico turned his head to smile at her. "You mean like a bird?"

"No." She giggled. "To fly a plane. To be a pilot gliding through the sky. No one to bother you. Complete freedom."

Nico didn't want to remind her that just that morning, she skinned her knees falling down the steps of her grandparents' house. He couldn't resist gently teasing her. "Georgie, sometimes, you have trouble navigating things on land. I'm not quite sure about the sky!"

Georgie turned and pushed his shoulder, a reluctant smile on her face. She sighed. "You're right, I know. But I'd love to try!"

They had laughed and moved on to other subjects, but Nico was secretly glad she confided something in him. He desperately wanted to kiss her, but he struggled to be a gentleman all summer. Perhaps it was the time spent with Piero, but Nico was intent on not taking advantage of Georgie's inexperience. The weeks flew, and it was only when she mentioned there was only a week left before she would return home that Nico panicked.

Their first kiss was so very sweet but also awkward. They were picking lemons, and Nico found himself watching Georgie all day. She was working hard alongside everyone else, picking baskets of lemons that got transferred to crates and then added to pallets. They were taking a break, sitting in the clearing near the stone building that housed tools. Fortunately, for once, no one was around. He had taken her by surprise, swooping in quickly to kiss her soft pink lips. She was shocked, but immediately responded until they both backed away, their eyes wide. They laughed about it later, agreeing their second kiss was far more romantic. It occurred under the twinkling stars as they walked through the lemon grove.

After that, they spent every available second together, and when Georgie left, she had tears in her eyes. They began writing to each other, long emails of dreams, sharing their most cherished secrets. He read each of them over a hundred times and kept them in a secret electronic folder. As he bent over his computer, the relentless teasing from his brothers echoed in his ears. They only ceased after their mother shushed them, obviously seeing the look of joy on his face when a new email arrived.

Nico arrived in Sicily way before Georgie the next summer. Spending considerable time with Piero again earned the man's trust—almost. Piero still had some reservations about entrusting his only granddaughter to a young man, regardless of how much he liked him.

It took a lot of persuasion, but Nico was finally given permission to drive to Palermo to meet Georgie at the airport. He was instructed to pick her up and drive straight home to Nizza. She exited customs to glance around, and when her gaze finally centered on him, she opened her sweet mouth in a giant shriek of surprise. No one shrieked better than Georgie. Then she ran to him, tripping over her suitcase and landing flat on her face. His sweet, clumsy Georgie. If he had any doubts about her sustained love for him, they dissipated with her enthusiastic hug and kisses once he was able to pull her upright. It was all they could do to get to the car to have some private time. Their kisses were hot and urgent, and he purposely drew away, his heart thudding. Warnings from his mother, his brothers and even Piero were ingrained in his head and he could not take advantage of the situation, but oh, did he want to. But Georgie deserved so much more than rolling around in the car. He finally composed himself enough to drive her to Nizza. There were two or three small stops along the way, but he contained himself.

That summer was bittersweet torture. They knew before it even started that they would have less time together. Georgie had been accepted into the University of St. Andrews in Scotland. Freshies, as she called it, began near the end of August, but prior to that, she needed to return home to pack. She warned him it meant departing by mid-August.

The worry of her going to university had already started to consume Nico. He still had a year left in the Italian education system and then he would take his graduation exams. From there, he would need to follow in his brothers' footsteps and attend a university in the States. *Zio* Angelo demanded an American education for them due to the global nature of their business. Already, Nico did not want to go, knowing it would be even farther from Georgie.

When he tried to bring up the subject of university to Georgie, she told him she didn't want to focus on it. It was important to just concentrate on their time together. The sunny days in Sicily that summer passed by as quickly as turning pages of a book. Nico spent his days working on Piero's farms, cultivating the soil. He listened to the older man tell him the land was everything. It was the center of the community. Their livelihood not only helped them, but it flowed down in so many ways, from the laborers in his fields to those who bought his lemons to make lemon *granita*, limoncello, and other products. Piero felt they single-handedly were responsible for the economy of the small *comune* of Nizza, even if that was an exaggeration. He was proud of his farm and enthusiastically shared his passion.

At night, Nico usually dined with Georgie and her grandparents before going to sit with her on the veranda or take long walks in the fields. On weekends, sometimes they went to the beach, where they sat on the pebbled filled sand and watched the color of the Ionian Sea change to become almost clear as it neared the shore. Nico would often swim or snorkel in the crystal blue water while Georgie lounged on the water's edge. Most times, they would get distracted, wrapped up in each other.

Nico began to feel like there was never a time he didn't know Georgie. He spilled his heart to her, telling her private thoughts and feelings he had never shared with anyone. Whenever he was with her, he experienced a mix of vulnerability and strength, knowing he could trust her unconditionally.

By now, the other boys he once worked with had matured as well. Once or twice, he found one of them approaching Georgie while she hung laundry for *Nonna* or drove lunch to *Nonno* in the fields. It was true that Georgie had not flirted or even sought that attention. If at all, she seemed unaware of their advances. Nico took care of those potential suitors privately. He was not subtle about it. In fact, he felt somewhat caveman like, but his protectiveness of Georgie was something he never felt before.

Looking at her now as an adult woman gazing into the fields, he was reminded of that eighteen-year-old girl he watched walk away in the Palermo Airport, while his heart broke in pieces. Prior to her departure, Piero allowed them to spend the day together in the city before her evening flight. It had been so wonderful to experience Palermo with Georgie. Nico had only been there twice and found Sicily's capital to be vibrant and rich in history. It was a colorful blend of so many architectural styles of past civilizations. Trying to remember his history, he explained to Georgie the influence of the Phoenicians, Greeks, Arabs, Normans, Romans and Spanish and all the traditions that they brought.

It had been a magical day taking in the rugged city, where old palaces and churches mingled with modern cafes and stores catering to visitors. When they came out of the Palermo Cathedral, which Georgie had explored thoroughly, they found themselves in driving rain and wind. They soon learned her flight was canceled, but they were able to find a hotel room for the night. Nico swallowed hard, remembering that night spent together. He could have exploited the good fortune but knowing he would have to drive back and face Piero held him back. They argued, for Georgie had felt rejected and couldn't understand the man he was trying to be. Once daylight dawned, he drove her to the airport, filled with a mixture of pride and regret. Letting her go had been the hardest thing he had ever done. They both vowed to somehow make the distance work and to be honest with each other. He had meant it, but now he realized it was only the dream of youth.

GEORGIE KNOCKED over her glass of water and the crash startled Nico out of his thoughts. He instantly grabbed his napkin to help her wipe up the liquid. She gave him a small smile. "Sorry, I don't know why I'm so clumsy today."

He couldn't help but almost grin. That part of her stayed unchanged throughout the years. Though she looked like the young Georgie, she also appeared different. Her once waist-length curly hair was now shoulder length, and it looked like she straightened its tight curls to waves around her shoulders. Of course, her eyes did not hold the love they once did. She had an edge now that wasn't apparent in her youth.

The wind blew her hair, and she brushed it impatiently behind her ear. Her expression displayed a sadness he had never seen. Grief was a terrible monster, and Piero's death affected them both. He felt compelled to say something. "Georgie, I hope you know *Nonno* was ready to go. We talked a lot about his wishes. Even though he didn't tell me he was sick, he said life just wasn't the same after *Nonna* died."

She turned to stare at him. Her dark blue eyes seemed to bore into him. "Where were you?"

He was confused. "When?"

She appeared to swallow hard. She stood abruptly, her hands

on her hips. "You always act like my grandparents meant so much to you. Where were you last year when *Nonna* died?"

Georgie stared at Nico, waiting for his answer. It took a couple hours, but now she was over the nervousness of seeing him again and the terms of the will had sunk in. She wasn't sure how she felt about everything. For some reason, her anger was rising. Was this sudden rage directed at *Nonno* dying or was it because Nico got half of what should be hers? After all, she was family. She was blood. Nico was... What actually was he?

Inhaling deeply, her breath caught in her throat as she remembered her grandmother's funeral. Torn with grief, she was angry when her heart betrayed her, beating wildly in anticipation of seeing Nico again. She felt the weight of guilt creeping in, but she couldn't control her thoughts that his physical presence would bring comfort to her. But all her emotions were unnecessary; there was nothing but an enormous bouquet from Nico's mother, Margherita. The card made it clear that it was from the whole family. And Nico never arrived. He did not show up for her when he knew Georgie needed him.

He looked chagrined now, almost as if she had caught him at something. "I would have liked to have been here. Unfortunately, I was in the states studying for my advanced degree," he said cooly. "*Nonno* understood. He should have told you."

Georgie stared at him without blinking. "He told me," she admitted flatly.

"Well, if he told you, then why are you asking me?"

She raised an eyebrow at his mocking tone. She didn't know this Nico. He was so cold. Clearly, he had changed, and now she was stuck with him. It would have been easier to share the land with anyone else but him.

Rather than answer, she began gathering up their plates, and he made a move to help her. She purposely put a hand up, signaling that she could do it herself. For the first time, he appeared unsure, his usually confident demeanor wavering. She was tired of this game they were playing, yet she wasn't going to be the first one to crack. If he wanted to pretend they were acquaintances and no more, so could she. Staring at her, he thanked her politely for lunch. Nodding, she carried the plates inside and put them on the counter, lost in thought. When she heard his voice, she jumped.

Whirling around, she shrieked, "You scared me!"

Why was there humor in his eyes? What was funny about scaring her? He seemed to be biting back his smile. "*Mi dispiace.* It's just your shriek. No one else I know screams in that octave that you are able to achieve."

She rolled her eyes and pretended to be busy putting away the ingredients she had gotten out to make the pancakes.

"I was asking if you wanted to talk about where we go from here as co-owners."

She shook her head and didn't turn around before answering. "Not really. Perhaps we can when the *festa* is over. I need to focus on that for now."

"But we should probably at least address it," he argued, speaking from behind her. She wanted more than anything to turn around and bury herself in his powerful arms like she did as a teenager. In the past, his long, comforting hugs had a way of making all her problems disappear. Instead, now she straightened her back and began to wash the dishes. Since it was the two of them, that didn't take long. She dried her hands on the dish towel and finally turned around. He was leaning against her grandmother's old-fashioned table, the one she used daily for making pasta. Georgie swallowed hard at the memory, avoiding Nico's gaze, which she found unnerving. She stared at his chest instead.

"The *festa* is the most important thing right now. I need to concentrate on that. Afterward, we can talk and sort out how this is going to work," she said more calmly than she felt. Trying to appear confident, she finally let her gaze finally travel up to his. "Thank you for coming. If you don't mind, I think I'm going to take a nap. It's been a tough few days."

Giving him her polite, but distant smile, the one she had long perfected for her parents' friends and work associates, she indicated the door. "Please show yourself out," she said as she edged past him, trying to appear dignified while being careful not to touch him. It was only when she closed the door to her bedroom that she crumbled and let her grief for so many things pour out.

four

Georgie sat on the veranda with her legs tucked under her for warmth. The early morning hours had arrived, but sleep eluded her, leaving her feeling restless. Rising to watch the sky light up from the sunrise over the vast lemon grove was a decision that came easily. She sipped her tea and tried to soak in the calmness of the early morning.

Tossing and turning all night, her dreams returned to Nico. Except now, her memories were a chaotic blur of the old and new Nico—the boy versus the man. She didn't know where one left off and the other began. Her sadness began to turn to anger. How dare he hijack her grief? This was a time for her to honor her grandfather, reminisce about her grandmother, and fully embrace the profound sense of loss she felt. Her heart ached with the weight of sadness. For some reason, she always believed her grandparents were untouchable, like superheroes. They were the one presence in her life she always counted on, and now they were gone. It felt like someone had taken her world, shook it hard and then tipped her out into an abyss.

This was her time to wallow in self-pity. But what was she doing? Tossing and turning over a man. Grunting in disgust, she proclaimed out loud, "He's not worth it," to the empty veranda. Why should she even give Nico a second thought? For the most part, he treated her so coldly. Yesterday, there were occasional cracks in his demeanor, and she saw the anguish in his eyes over her grandfather's death. If she mentally took the high road, she would excuse some of his behavior to his own grief. Stubbornly, she fought down any sense of reason. After all, it was her grandfather, her blood. Her own grief should take priority.

Georgie rocked back in his chair and stroked its arm with a gentle hand. How often had she sat on the veranda's stairs and watched *Nonno* rock in his chair? Georgie had seen the loneliness in his eyes and felt helpless after her grandmother's death. Deep in her heart, she always knew he might die soon, but finding it too difficult to contemplate, she remained in denial.

Why did he tie her to Nico in such a permanent way? *Nonno* must have known there was no way she could ever part with the land. And stubborn Nico probably was going to feel the same. Now they were stuck together forever. And it wasn't like he needed more property. His family owned half of Sicily from what she heard. She looked down at the small framed photo she had found in the spare bedroom that her grandparents once told her was reserved only for her. While she had seen the photo a thousand times, it hit her like a lightning bolt last night. The photo of her and Nico the summer she turned eighteen captured a magical moment. It was taken in the lemon fields in the golden hour, when the sun was deep into the horizon and the light reflecting off the trees was at its finest. She was looking directly at the camera, but Nico, with his arms around her from behind, was staring intently at her, his fine chiseled cheekbones prominent. The photo didn't show his eyes, but she imagined the love in them. Her hands were holding onto his muscular arms, and her face glowed.

Georgie smiled gently at the photo, her finger tracing their images. Two naïve kids who thought somehow their love could make it, despite the odds. Their innocence radiated from the fading photo. She had been so sheltered when she first met him. Assuming he was a laborer, she thought he was one of the local kids who came to make money in the summer to help their families. Often, those kids and their fathers worked alongside each other in the same fields. It surprised her to learn that Nico actually lived outside Positano on the Amalfi Coast and his uncle was a good friend of her grandfather's. Nico had been sent to their farm not only to work, but to learn.

It was only after she and Nico grew close that he confided his uncle was very wealthy, owned a significant amount of property in southern Italy and Sicily, and ran a global export company centered on products made from lemons and olive oil. As a teenager, she dismissed it as inconsequential. Being from a wealthy background herself, she was accustomed to associating with affluent individuals. Nico made it very clear, though, that it was his uncle's wealth. He rarely talked about his own father, who had left his mother, only stating flatly that he hardly remembered him. Instead, Nico always managed to draw her out, hanging onto her every word with genuine interest.

Now sitting on the veranda, Georgie rubbed her tired eyes. Nico's kindness toward her as a teenager was particularly striking, especially considering the lack of emotion she observed in her own household. Her father, George, had always made it plain he had wanted a son. Since her mother's pregnancy was difficult, the couple agreed they would only have one child, so Georgie became his namesake. A career military officer, he demonstrated little emotion at home. He was strict, exacting and often said he did not suffer fools gladly.

George, a staunch English gentleman, came from a respectable background, and seemed so very different from her diminutive Italian mother, Elena. Elena had earned a scholarship to Oxford, where she immersed herself in English literature. She loved it so much that she found herself absorbed in the

English culture. At Oxford, she made many friends, one being a well-bred daughter of an Earl who also happened to be a Goddaughter of the Queen. This introduced Elena into exclusive English circles. It was during a weekend house party that fate brought her parents together.

No one ever discussed Georgie's Italian heritage, even though she was aware of it. Raised as a proper English young lady with a nanny, she grew up at their home in Hertfordshire, a village of Radlett, northwest of the center of London. Elena, now a prominent professor of English Literature at Oxford, demonstrated her love in her own way. She frequently became sidetracked, however, her attention consumed by the captivating world of books. Georgie eventually grew accustomed to it as a normal part of their relationship. On Georgie's tenth birthday, Elena sat her down and gently broke the news that she would be spending her summer holiday with her grandparents in Sicily. Elena traveled with Georgie for the first holiday. The stilted conversation between her mother and grandparents was almost painful, and Georgie had not wanted to stay. In fact, after her mother departed, it was only the delicious aromas coming from the kitchen that finally lured her out of her bedroom.

Thinking back, Georgie remembered how patient her grandparents were. They let her settle in, absorbing her into their household contently. Slowly Georgie began to learn Italian, and they often laughed good-naturedly at her accent. Encouraged and nurtured by both, she was given chores that she embraced. She would do anything to help these strong, independent people. In the evenings, they lingered over long dinners where they told her about her great-grandparents and their own childhoods.

Summers were eagerly awaited from then on. After the first visit, she traveled alone. Her parents rarely asked many questions about her time in Sicily, and Georgie learned quickly not to offer. Every year, she arrived back in England nicely tanned and bursting with excitement about the happenings at the farm, only to tamp them down when she saw her parents' frowns at any mention of her time there.

Things changed when Nico and she became involved. Her mother overhead a late-night whispered call and asked questions. When Georgie offered little information, an angry phone call to her grandmother followed. Elena was clearly questioning her grandmother about Georgie being allowed to be around "some farmer." Eventually, her mother's uneasiness subsided, but Georgie became adept at being discreet to avoid any future confrontation.

Georgie grimaced now, thinking back to that time. Compliant and innocent, she allowed her parents to select her university, remarkably in Scotland no less. She naively believed that she could keep Nico as a cherished presence in her life.

However, once at university, she found a surprising feeling of freedom she had never felt before. Normally shy, except with Nico, she was forced to come out of her shell quickly. Her roommates helped her buy clothes that were more sophisticated than she usually wore. She experimented with makeup and different hairstyles. There were parties and social events where she made even more friends, including boys.

Trying to keep up with her studies was also challenging. Emails to Nico, once a priority, slackened a bit. She was still in love with him, but deep down she felt a sense of liberation she couldn't even express to him. He would not understand. Sensing her withdrawal, Nico seemed to cling tighter, wanting and needing more from her. Looking back, Georgie could see that she was not only rebelling from her parents but also the unintentional pressure she felt from Nico. Finally, she could live her life without the constant weight of others' expectations.

Resisting the offers of dates for the first several months, she confidently assured her friends that she was in love with her boyfriend. Despite admiring the photos of the handsome Italian young man that adorned her Hall of Residence, known as St.

Salvator's Hall or Sallies. The girls made fun of her decision to isolate herself from the university's social life.

They didn't laugh quite as hard when Nico arrived in the flesh. Surprising her as she walked out of class on a Friday, she tripped into his outstretched arms. Proudly, she brought him to a big party that night, where her girlfriends gushed over him. A tremendously good-looking foreigner was not lost on her friends and Georgie frowned, as she almost had to fight them off. Though Nico dressed in jeans, a casual shirt and a leather jacket, for some reason he didn't look as refined as the boys attending the university. Their attire spoke of sophistication, with khaki trousers and neatly pressed button-down shirts and pullovers. Jealous of the attention Nico was receiving, they snickered obviously at him from the corner. It was a relief when Nico left for his hotel room, telling her he was tired from the trip.

The next day was better, with just the two of them slipping away for a quiet picnic. However, the rain and wind quickly forced them back inside. As they indulged in stolen kisses in her bustling room, the spark of their passion lacked its usual intensity. Finally, she pushed away from him, suggesting brightly that they go to the local pub where everyone was likely gathering. It was loud and music blared as students drank pitchers of beer and danced. Her friends begged her to stay, but she could see how uncomfortable Nico was watching the boys get inebriated and the girls dance almost obscenely with their chosen boy for the evening. He even raised his eyebrows at Georgie's short skirt and crop top. "Is that how you dress now?" he asked, making him sound like an aging uncle. Frowning at him, she had instead danced with her girlfriends, watching with a glare as girls approached him at the bar. Eventually, he asked her to dance, but she could tell he was uncomfortable and by mutual agreement, he took her back to Sallies. Her roommate, who didn't like to party, was inside, already asleep. Georgie suggested they go back to his hotel room, but he politely declined, his eyes wary.

The next day, his silence spoke volumes as they rode silently in the taxi to the airport. Georgie rushed to fill the awkwardness, rambling on about topics that she knew held no interest for him. He looked uncertain and vulnerable, and she rushed to reassure him with long hugs and kisses. Before walking away, he cast an uncertain glance at her, his eyes searching for answers. Watching his back as he departed, she bit her lip, a gnawing awareness of doom growing inside her.

It was soon after that Henry appeared. He had a quick smile and a sense of humor that endeared him to her during their history class. He became her partner on assignments, much to the dismay of several girls who craved that same opportunity. Georgie knew she was the subject of their envy, and she was flattered that Henry sought her out.

When he finally asked her to an upcoming party, she told him she needed to think about it. She still remembered the conversation with Nico. After careful rehearsal, she called him to suggest they date other people. How could they both get through university life without doing so? After all, he must have met girls he would like to get to know. They could remain friends and reconnect again after university.

Deep down, she knew her suggestion wouldn't go over well with Nico, and she had been right. Their discussion included long silences on his end, and it was obvious he wasn't going to make it easy. Finally, he thanked her for her honesty and hung up. Initially, she felt awful, yet strangely free. Didn't he understand they both needed to explore? How would they ever know if they were meant for each other if they didn't see other people?

She went out with Henry a few times. It only took a brief amount of time for her to realize Henry was more in love with Henry. Next came James, or was it John? A long list of guys followed. Georgie never could figure out why no one seemed to spark her heart. She tried to call Nico a few times, but he never picked up. One rainy Sunday after a particularly raucous

Saturday night, she felt a loneliness set in. Unsure of herself, she reached out to who she believed was her friend. She wrote him a long email, pouring out her feelings, including the uncertainty, her wish that they could somehow make it work. It went unanswered. Eventually, the photos of him were taken down, and her feelings were shoved into the recesses of her heart. She sighed now, thinking of it.

"What are you doing with *that*?"

Georgie blinked, startled, as she was so lost in the past. She turned to see Nico standing on the porch, staring with a dark gaze at the frame in her hands.

five

Nico couldn't take his eyes off the photo Georgie was holding. Where did it come from, and why was she looking at it now? Sure, they had a lot of memories together. But there was a big part of him that couldn't let those emotions in—not again. He often wondered if this was how his mother felt after his father left. Hardly a fair comparison, given that his parents were married and had three children together. He and Georgie had been teenage crushes, nothing more. Of course, at the time, he swore it was true love. But the ease at which she moved on had been startling after their awkward weekend together.

He remembered the phone call like it was yesterday. She stumbled over her words, like she usually did with her feet. It was uncharacteristic for his precise-speaking Georgie. Before she started to talk, he knew what she was about to say. In fact, he had been expecting it for weeks. Despite that, it was like someone sticking a knife slowly into him. Though rationally, he knew the issues with their relationship were not black and white, he deliberately made it so in his head. He felt utterly abandoned.

Eventually, he moved on—he had to. It had been extremely difficult not to email her back when later she wrote and told him of her confused feelings, but he refused to be jerked around like a puppet. Once he arrived at Stanford, he assumed his feelings would dissipate. Marco had convinced him to go to his alma mater, and Nico, feeling indifferent, surprisingly agreed without objection. Attending an American university was what his *Zio* Angelo wanted. It wasn't Nico's dream. Choosing to study business, Nico assumed he would be thrust into his family's company and gave no real thought to what he really wanted to do.

He dated and partied at every opportunity. So much so that his grades slipped to the point that he was almost sent home. Realizing the disappointment that would come from his family, Nico resolved to find a balance. It depressed him to realize that no girl came close to Georgie. Oh, he tried to find someone who did, that's for sure. He felt a pang of guilt as he reflected on the multitude of hearts he callously broke. It wasn't fair to the women he dated. Yet Nico was the eternal optimist, hoping there was someone who would fill his heart as Georgie had.

Because Stanford had a host of international students, he kept up with Georgie's life by reading the London tabloids at the newsstand on campus. Photos of Georgie out enjoying London's nightlife with the British aristocracy and wanna-be's seemed to be great fodder for paparazzi. Perhaps it was her wild blonde hair or the way her beautiful face lit up any room, but their lenses were trained on her even more than some of the more famous people she was with.

He bought the newspapers and took them to his room to absorb. His hope was that at some point, he would finally be able to acknowledge their different worlds and move on. Those photos always led to a crazy night of partying, and the next day, he woke bleary-eyed, with a heavy heart, swearing he wouldn't do it again. And hit repeat.

After graduation, it was *Zio* Angelo who intervened, getting him back on track. Angelo insisted Nico follow his passion for the land, giving him the responsibility of overseeing their vast number of farms. While it left him no time for working in the soil, it at least allowed him to stay away from the business side of the company.

Angelo's death shocked them all. As Marco dove into his new responsibility, Nico found himself almost pulling away, realizing life was short. He spent more and more time in his beloved greenhouses. It was his mother who finally suggested he go back to the states and get advanced degrees and certifications in agricultural science. He returned to Northern California to the land that was also ravaged by the effects of the climate. There, he realized with incredulity how much farther he was in the understanding and science of regenerative farming. His own instructors asked him probing questions. Still, he eventually gained new knowledge that sent him back to Italy with more confidence.

The abrupt sound of Georgie placing the photo face down on the table startled him back to reality. Their image no longer stared at them. She was assessing him, her gaze traveling to his faded jeans and white polo shirt. "What do you want, Nico?"

Now it was he who felt uncertain. "I...er, Luciano called. Apparently, there was a paper he forgot to have us sign. I texted you about it an hour or so ago."

She reached up unconsciously to run a hand through her hair. Today, it was back to its wild self, its corkscrews untamed. She was wearing shorts that exposed her long legs, and her action to grab her hair made her shirt ride up, exposing her midriff. He swallowed hard and tried to look away but found he couldn't.

"My phone is still on the charger. I'm sorry. The morning got away from me. I'll get changed, and we can wait for him."

Nico stared at her. "I told him he didn't have to come up the hill to the house. We'd meet him in town."

Confusion flitted across her features, almost as if she wanted to ask him something. Instead, she stood. "I will be right back."

As she brushed past, he tried not to inhale, but it was futile. He smelled the lavender soap she used and whatever other scent from her hair. Whatever it was, remained the same from so long ago. It brought him right back to the past. He shook his head as if to clear it as she went inside. She was probably wondering why he didn't tell her to meet him in town. Truthfully, when she didn't answer her phone that morning, he became nervous. He wasn't thrilled she was up on the remote hill all alone. Especially if word got out around the small town that she had a sizeable inheritance. Men always flocked to Georgie—now there would be a wolf pack at her door. They would not know she was married. Nor would they really care if they thought they had some kind of chance. He frowned. It was no business of his, but he needed to protect her. He owed *Nonno* that, at the very least.

When she entered a few minutes later, his heartbeat quickened. Dressed in a light pink-colored sundress, she was chic and fresh at the same time. Her curly hair was now in a low ponytail, which accentuated her cheekbones. Standing before him, she smiled tentatively at him.

He said the first thing that came to his mind. "Call your husband. He needs to come stay with you."

She looked at him quizzically. "My husband?"

"Duke Benjamin or whatever the hell his name is. Call him and tell him to get his butt on a plane and be here for you. You shouldn't be up here alone."

She opened her mouth and closed it again. Her eyes were shooting daggers at him. "Benjamin will not be joining me," she said, annunciating each word.

He glanced at her ringless hand, and his eyebrows went up.

Was she wearing a ring yesterday? He hadn't even noticed in his shock over Piero's death.

"Then pack your bags. You're coming home with me."

"Are you mad? I'm not going anywhere with you! Why on earth would I?" Georgie exclaimed in surprise. Her tone indicated she almost dared him to order her around.

"Georgie, you shouldn't be staying here alone! You're isolated up here."

She rolled her enormous blue eyes. "Is there a crime wave in Nizza that I'm not aware of?"

Nico frowned. "Of course not, but every male around here is going to start sniffing around. They'll hear you inherited the farm and will entertain the thought of becoming land barons of their own by seducing you."

"You are being dramatic! Nico, I am remaining here. Alone," she said succinctly.

Frowning at her, he realized she wasn't going to make this easy. But Georgie never made anything easy in his life. He glanced at his watch. "Fine. Right now, we don't have time to argue. Luciano is expecting us soon."

"I'm ready," she said pointedly.

"Then let's go," he snapped.

Getting into his Jeep, he instantly put on his sunglasses, and Georgie did the same. They wound down the hill without speaking, driving into the quiet center of Nizza. Luciano had texted him to come to a local café instead of his office. Nico pulled in front of it and snapped off his seatbelt in silence.

"I thought he wanted us to meet him at his office."

"He wants to meet here," Nico responded shortly.

Getting out, his manners automatically directed him to go to her side of the vehicle. Georgie carefully jumped out, as if she was worried about tripping. But now she was frowning at the café. Did she remember its significance? When her grandparents finally consented to him taking her on a date, he brought her to this small eatery. Owned by Maurizio and Josephine, it was hardly private. The realization had hit Nico that their every action would be meticulously reported back to Georgie's doting grandparents.

Now, like most of Nizza, the café looked the same as it had for decades. The sense of timelessness of the town struck Nico and he enjoyed the familiarity it usually brought. However, he realized that today would not be a day for those nostalgic feelings.

"Georgie!" exclaimed Josephine as they entered the restaurant. Now older and grayer, Josephine encircled Georgie in a bear hug, whispering to her in Italian, tears in her eyes. Georgie nodded back, obviously overcome. Instantly, guilt washed over Nico. For a few minutes, he forgot the grief they were both experiencing. He needed to put aside his feelings from the past—especially her marriage—and be cordial, at the very least.

Extricating Georgie from Josephine's iron grip, Nico kissed the older woman as well and led Georgie over to a small table by the window. The town's residents were glancing over surreptitiously, but Nico shrugged it off. They probably had heard gossip by now and it was useless to even address it.

They sat down at the table, and Georgie played with the salt and pepper shakers. Her delicate hands moved them around the table. He indicated her left hand.

"You don't wear a ring?"

She shook her head and remained silent.

"A woman should wear a wedding ring. Especially in this town. Without it, people will talk."

Georgie's eyes widened, clearly taken aback by his unfamiliar formal tone. He probably sounded like he was eighty years old. Josephine appeared just in time, setting glass bowls of refreshing lemon *granita* in front of them and a plate of Savoiardi, delicately powdered Sicilian cookies. They both stared at the food.

"Did you plan this?" Georgie asked accusingly.

He decided to play dumb. "Plan what?"

"Nico, you know what!" Georgie hissed at him. "This is where we came on our first date. And this is what we ate!"

He couldn't help the small smile that came over him. "I remember," he acknowledged. He softened his tone. "But I didn't plan it, Georgie. Honestly."

She nodded and looked away. Was she crying? He couldn't tell from her averted gaze.

"I am sorry I snapped at you earlier as well," he said gently. "We are both grieving, and I promise I will remember that. Obviously, he was your grandfather, not mine. And though I loved him, I know how much he meant to you. Maybe we should call a truce and at least try to keep things civil to honor him."

She nodded, saying nothing. Picking up her spoon, she took a spoonful of the frozen lemon ice and sighed, her eyes closed. "Just like I remembered. It is amazing."

He couldn't take his eyes off her beautiful face. Even with her eyes closed and no makeup, she was breathtaking. Her curved eyebrows perfectly highlighted her enormous eyes. She had the most gorgeous pink lips. He remembered the taste of them like it was yesterday.

Swallowing hard, he savored the icy sweetness of his own *granita*. He wished he was anywhere but there. This was too difficult. Punching something right now would feel better than sitting calmly pretending to enjoy a lemon *granita*. He wondered what the other patrons would do if he hurled the plate of cookies at the wall like he wanted to? Eating his *granita* too fast, he got a brain freeze. Dropping his spoon, he wiped his mouth with a napkin and tried to approach Georgie again.

"Is your husband coming to the *festa*? At least you won't be living alone too long."

She shook her head as she bit into a cookie with her perfect white teeth. She chewed it, staring at him. She swallowed and finally spoke softly. "I don't have a husband."

His eyebrows rose. "Divorced already?"

"I never got married," she answered dully.

"But I saw you. I mean, of course you did!" Nico exclaimed louder than he intended.

"*Mi dispiace*. My court case ran long." Luciano sat down at their table, looking uncomfortable, staring at their dark expressions.

"My goodness, that *granita* looks delicious," he remarked with a false sense of cheer.

six

Georgie took another bite with a calmness she didn't feel. Why did Nico think she was married? More importantly, how did he even know she *almost* got married?

It wasn't that long ago that she met Benjamin, but it seemed like a distant memory. Nico was right. He was officially a duke after the recent death of his father. Prior to meeting him, Georgie had been floundering. It was after university when she became aware of her parents' persistent thoughts about her getting married. In fact, her father went so far as to name several potential suitors. Georgie pictured herself in some Victorian novel. Alarmed, she found herself going out partying at night—anything to prevent finding another new prospective date at the dinner table. Soon, she realized she wasn't used to London's nightlife, which was like her university days on steroids. Out of her depth, she often found herself in awkward situations, and the press loved it. Admittedly, she drank too much, stayed out too late and ran with the in crowd.

To say her parents were less than pleased was an understatement. She was told in no uncertain terms to find a job and a flat. Georgie quietly agreed and was pleased when she found employment so soon. Much later, she discovered that the job she believed she had earned on her own was actually arranged by her father. Serving as a personal assistant to a venture capitalist, she tried to tell herself she enjoyed that line of work. After a day that would drag on endlessly, she went out with her friends. To return to her posh flat meant feeling the loneliness. She tried to stuff it down. It felt as if life was going by in slow motion, and not in a good way. Time passed, and she continued existing. She became worn down by it all, and over a rare lunch with her mother, it was Elena who suggested quietly that she needed to find her passion. Elena spoke of her own desires, the love of literature. While Georgie respected her mother's career, she knew she didn't share anything near that dream.

The conversation left Georgie reeling. What was her passion? Her mother struck a nerve within her, and for some time, Georgie truly wondered if she was passionate about anything. She traveled to see her grandparents, hoping they would spark something. While she loved it there, and they truly believed in her, there really was not a place for her there, either.

Deep in thought, she walked the fields and breathed in the soil and scents coming off the bushes. Harvest had already occurred, and just a few lemons were left dangling from the branches. She picked one and breathed in its delicious, sweet scent. It was amazing how smells could transport you back to a time and place. Instantly, she was the awkward sixteen-year-old coming face to face with the most beautiful young man she had ever seen. Remembering how passionate Nico was about the land made her even more wishful.

Suddenly, she wanted to see him. Maybe she didn't know what her passion was in regard to career, but she had memories of being passionate. Did she still have any of those feelings? All she knew was that when she was with Nico, he always helped her sort out her feelings. She wondered briefly if it was a longing for those summers when life had been so simple and sweet.

Instantly dismissing that idea, she realized Nico still had a piece of her heart that she hadn't given to anyone. It would be wonderful to see him and at least find out if he felt any feelings toward her anymore.

Swallowing her pride was the most difficult thing she had ever done. Her grandparents hadn't questioned her at all, but she saw the glint in *Nonno*'s eyes when she told them where she was going. It was a quick flight from Palermo to Naples, where she then hired a driver to take her to Nico's home.

As the car curved up the drive to the immense white farmhouse in the family's estate, she felt her heart almost stop beating. What if he rejected her? Worse, what if he no longer felt anything for her? Perhaps he was already engaged or committed to another woman? How vain and conceited she was to think he would still even want to have anything to do with her after she brushed him off years prior. How self-absorbed she was to think she could just drop in and have him sort out her future.

The car stopped on the circular entrance in front of the home, and the driver held the door open for her. Instantly, Georgie opened her mouth to tell him to take her back to Naples. This had been a ridiculously horrible idea. She glanced at the grand house with its balconies and curved windows. Lights glowed in every window as dusk settled. Despite its size, it looked like a well-loved home.

With her legs feeling frozen, she gave the driver a panicked look. He returned her gaze with a confused one of his own. She cleared her throat, formulating in her head the Italian it would require explaining she no longer wanted to go inside.

Her heart rate increased drastically and was beating out of her chest. It was only out of the corner of her eye that she realized the front door had swung open. A woman was coming down the stairs, smiling a little at her. The woman had dark hair wrapped in a ponytail. She was exquisitely dressed in black pants and a navy silk blouse. Staring at her, Georgie tried to mask her terror.

"*Buonasera*. You must be Georgina," the woman said, smiling widely.

"Uh, yes?" Georgie winced, realizing she had answered her as if it was a question. She tried again. "Yes, yes, I am. But how did you know...?" She trailed off.

The woman came closer now and stooped to kiss each of her cheeks. She drew back and smiled. "I could spot the woman my son is in love with anywhere."

"GEORGIE, LUCIANO IS WAITING," Nico said quietly.

She blinked back to the present. "Oh, sorry. I was just thinking about something," she mumbled.

Luciano nodded understandingly. "Of course, you are remembering your grandfather," he said, finishing his *granita* with a flourish, and tossing his spoon into the small glass "Such a loss for all of us." Handing her a pen, he showed her the line she needed to sign. Nico had already done so. She signed and handed the pen back, and Luciano stood and gathered the papers.

"These will be filed with the court, and we won't have much left to do except tie up a few loose ends," he said.

Georgie watched Nico stand to embrace the older man, and she stood as well, kissing his weathered cheeks. "We will see you at the *festa*," she told him with a small smile. Watching him leave, she had an unreasonable wish to beg him to take her with him. The door's bell tinkled as he exited into the bright sunlight.

"Sit back down, Georgie," Nico ordered quietly.

"Stop bossing me around."

"We need to talk," he ground out.

"Fine," she snapped. Glancing around, she saw the interested gazes. "But let's get out of here, please."

Nico nodded, paying the bill, and after a prolonged goodbye to Josephine, they got back into the Jeep.

The last thing Georgie wanted to do was talk about Benjamin. She needed stalling time. "Nico, do you mind stopping at the farmer's market? I don't really have any groceries."

"We can't talk there," he said roughly.

"Look, I don't know why you're suddenly so interested in my personal life, but if you really want to know, as I told you, I am not married. I never got married."

"You ran out on him?"

She grimaced. "Something like that."

"Typical."

"What does that mean?" she asked, clearly annoyed.

He shook his head and muttered a few select Italian words.

"I know what you're saying," Georgie said quietly. "I know enough Italian, especially the swear words."

He glanced at her with his sunglasses on. She couldn't see his eyes. She dug in her purse and put her own ones on. Fair was fair.

He took a deep breath. "*Mi dispiace*. I apologize. You are right. It's none of my business."

Releasing the brake, he drove slowly down to the water where the farmers' market was flourishing. Swinging into a parking place, he was about to exit the car when she put a hand on his arm.

"What do you mean you saw? There were no photos of it. My father bought everything from the paparazzi."

He took off his sunglasses and looked at her squarely. "I was there."

~

GEORGIE STROLLED past the bustling stalls of the market. The fresh scents of beans, corn, tomatoes, and berries wafted through the air. As they kept walking, the pungent smell of fish greeted them. While her senses took it all in, Georgie's mind continued trying to unravel Nico's words from the car. After he admitted he had been at her wedding, he simply got out of the Jeep as if he uttered something innocuous, like a statement about the weather.

She should stop and buy some of the fresh produce, but she no longer cared about shopping. It was only when they got to a vendor selling wild strawberries that he turned to her. "How many cartons do you want?" he asked with a slight grin. Unfortunately, his sunglasses still hid his eyes.

A small smile tugged at the corners of her lips. He hadn't forgotten her fondness for Sicily's wild strawberries. As a teenager, he often brought her a basket, and they would sit on her grandparents' veranda and eat them out of the carton.

"Two, please," she answered automatically, and Nico gave the vendor money and took the berries, now tucked away safely in a bag.

"Nico, you wanted to talk, so let's talk," Georgie demanded quietly. He nodded, his face still impassive and indicated a stone bench tucked away from the stalls.

Sitting down, she took her glasses off and stared at him, waiting for him to speak.

He took a deep breath. "I wasn't at your wedding. I was... well, I was across the street," he finally mumbled.

Georgie felt the blood draining from her face. "What did you see?"

He turned to her and took his own sunglasses off, but his gaze didn't meet hers. He seemed fixated on a spot over her right ear. "I saw you enter the cathedral. You looked breathtaking, Georgie. Perfect, really. But also, for some reason different than how I imagined."

Georgie winced, remembering the arguments over the wedding dress that she had detested, as well as her mother's insistence that she wear a tiara with an up-do. She took a deep, steadying breath. "How did you even know I was getting married?"

"I can read," he retorted.

Georgie stared at him, her eyebrows raised. "Yes, I know you can read, Nico. But I wasn't aware you kept up with the British tabloids."

"Well, I did at the time," he muttered. "I don't know, Georgie. I couldn't even figure out why I was there. Certainly, the time I was in London before that was a terrible experience. I had no desire to step into the city again."

seven

Nico looked away from Georgie's curious expression. He felt her eyes on him, but he couldn't return the gaze. It was humiliating. *Dio*, he was so stupid. Why had he blurted it out that he had been there? It was difficult enough to explain. He would not admit to her that he stood outside the church for hours that day waiting for her. Waiting for what? To see for certain that she got married? To see her as a bride? To make himself feel the worst pain of his life? He hadn't understood it then, and he didn't understand it now.

With another slip of the tongue, he just told her he had been in London prior to her wedding. There was hope she would not ask about that, too. The first trip he was referring to had been a disaster. It occurred after Georgie's visit to his family's home. His mother had called him while he had been traveling with his brother Stefano, doing business in America. Margherita excitedly launched into a detailed story about her surprise guest. He was astounded in a way, but it was typical Georgie to do something impulsive and just show up on his doorstep. Of course, she had no idea that he was in the states.

Margherita's enthusiastic account of Georgie's kind and

graceful nature had been hard to endure. Furiously, he hung up the phone. Stefano pestered him for details, but he remained silently seething. It took him days to realize a good part of his anger was the regret that his mother met Georgie without him being present. For years, he wanted to introduce his mother to Georgie as someone more to him than an ex-childhood sweetheart. Yet, she had shown up and wormed her way obviously into his mother's heart while he hadn't even been in the same country.

When Nico arrived home, he was hopeful his mother wouldn't mention Georgie's visit. There was no such luck. She regaled him with the entire story yet again; this time in front of his brother. "And you should see that hair, Stefano. Blonde and curly. Masses of it," Margherita exclaimed. "And such a sweet girl. So polite. I loved her correct British accent. I made her stay the night, of course, but she left first thing in the morning. I'm sure she felt awkward. Of course, I tried to make her feel at home. She only told me she wanted to talk to you, but she never confided in me what sparked her suddenly coming here," Margherita continued.

The idea that his brothers would spare a discussion about Georgie's visit was only a passing fancy. Both Marco and Stefano brought up the subject with him, knowing how besotted he had been in the early days. Give her a second chance, Stefano argued. Georgie had been young and reasonably wanting to have a life at university. Marco convinced him it was probably better in the end for them that she insisted they part ways. But now, if she was ready and wanted to rekindle a relationship, perhaps it was worth at least a conversation.

Marco's lecture on second chances was ironic coming from him. He had a string of girlfriends at the time, following a failed relationship. Nico hadn't understood his brother's quest for true love until much later when Marco finally found Kate, his soulmate.

It had taken several months, but Nico felt the old hurt begin to melt away, along with his resolve. Maybe his brothers were right. He could at least talk to Georgie about it. When he left home with an overnight bag, his mother smiled, wishing him a pleasant journey. He arrived in London later than he wanted and went directly to Georgie's home before finding a hotel. Standing at the door of the expansive old rectory in a village he could barely pronounce, he suddenly questioned the idea. A man in dark pants and a white shirt answered the door and told him succinctly that Georgie did not live there. Nico asked for her new address, and the man frowned. It was then a tall, older gentleman appeared.

"I will resolve this, William. Thank you," he said to the man who opened the door. The older man clearly was assessing him. "So, you're the Italian."

Nico frowned slightly at the man's rudeness but held his ground. He held out his hand. "Good evening, sir. I assume you are Mr. Worthington? I am Niccolo Rinaldi, and I am looking for Georgie."

The man ignored his hand, and Nico slowly withdrew it, feeling foolish.

"Georgina," the man said, enunciating her name, "no longer lives here. She has her own flat. I assume if she wanted you to know where she lived, she would have provided you with her address."

"Uh, we have been out of touch," Nico remarked uncomfortably. He opened his mouth to say Georgie had traveled to his own home but thought the better of it. "I came to London to discuss a few matters with her."

"You've wasted your time, Mr. Rinaldi. I doubt Georgie will want to see you. She has become seriously involved with a man both her mother and I have high regard for."

Nico swallowed hard and nodded. "I understand."

He saw a glimmer of something cross the older man's face,

and a wry smile appeared. "If you're determined to see Georgina, I can tell you where she is tonight."

Nico had felt a sense of relief wash over him. "I would appreciate that, sir."

Georgie's father then listed the name of a well-known restaurant. Nico was familiar with it, remembering that Marco enjoyed entertaining clients there when he did business in London. Thanking Georgie's father politely, Nico turned to leave. Something compelled him to turn around and face the man again. He grinned at the thought that perhaps Georgie's father didn't think he was so bad. "I hope to see you again, sir."

GEORGIE TOOK a strawberry carton out of the bag and balanced it on her lap. Picking one of the small ripe berries, she ripped the stem off and popped it into her mouth, chewing slowly. She might as well have something to eat. Nico was miles away, staring off into space. Swallowing the sweet berry, she had a sense of déjà vu wash over her. How long ago it was that they shared them together, watching the dusk turn into evening? Taking in the sun's warmth now, she took a deep breath of the sea air. Watching people shop in the bustling market, browsing the stalls, made her feel bittersweet. It had always been her favorite thing to do with *Nonna*.

"Want one?" she asked, offering the carton toward him. That seemed to break him out of his spell. He shook his head roughly, but a small smile crossed his face.

"You and I went through a lot of berries together that one summer," he acknowledged softly.

She felt the color rise in her cheeks, and her heart started beating faster as his gaze met hers. "Nico, I..." she began.

"Tell me what happened at your wedding, Georgie."

She tore her gaze away from his. Taking another berry, she

slowly put it in her mouth to stall for time. Finally, brushing her hands on her jeans, she put the carton back in the bag and glanced at him.

"You were right. I ran away. That's me. Runaway Georgie. I am surprised you didn't see the headlines. It was all over the news. *Runaway Bride Ditches Duke at the Altar!* or something like that. It ran in every tabloid for days."

He shook his head. "I was on a self-proclaimed news blackout. I thought anything I read would have all the details about the wedding."

"You cared?" she asked, swallowing hard.

"Of course I did," he almost shouted.

She looked around, but the marketgoers were busy shopping and talking to vendors. No one was paying them any attention. "Despite everything?"

He shrugged. "I know. I must love punishment. I guess I just had to see you get married to get over you."

Tears welled in her eyes. Suddenly, she was the insecure sixteen-year-old girl. "And did you? Get over me, I mean?"

He stared at her with cold eyes. "Definitely."

eight

Georgie picked the bouquet of wildflowers in the field and tossed them into the basket she had brought with her. She attempted to block out the memories of the small bouquets Nico used to bring her when they were kids. It always made her smile. Initially, he thrust them shyly at her when he came to family dinners. Later, after seeing how much she adored them, the bouquets grew in size, and he proudly presented them as if they were hothouse flowers.

Shaking her head to clear it of memories, she tried to focus on the *festa*, which was to be held the next day. Her grandfather had been very specific about it being held near his most sacred land at the original lemon grove. Workers arrived earlier to set up the tables, chairs, and canopies. Some of the local women offered tablecloths, and Georgie was planning to arrange flowers for each table. A dance floor was being delivered, and Georgie had hired a band as well. Her grandfather had been very particular about the band. She almost laughed at the comparison of this party to the ones she was used to attending in England. And yet, she by far preferred this simple approach.

Much had been accomplished in the last three days, despite

her thoughts going back to her confrontation with Nico. After his declaration of feeling nothing for her, she had stood and announced it was time for her to shop. Nico willingly trailed after her and carried her purchases. Neither said much, and when he dropped her off at the house, he inquired politely if she needed any help with the *festa*. She took on the same tone as his and just as icily told him, "No, thank you. My mother will arrive soon."

In fact, Elena was expected at any minute. Georgie walked back toward the house with her heavy basket, feeling the weight of not just the flowers but the burden of her life. Sitting down on the step of the expansive veranda, she took a canning jar from the box she found in the pantry. She clipped the flowers and started to arrange the bouquets. They looked sweet, all nestled in the jars. Fingering the purple petals, she smiled a little. These bouquets couldn't be more different from the elegant, all-white expensive flowers that graced her wedding. Wincing, she wondered how much her father had paid for the flowers alone. They had been everywhere in the church. And her own bouquet had been enormous.

Yesterday, she would have willingly told Nico the entire story, but when he flatly declared how little interest he had in the subject, she pushed it aside. He apparently didn't want to hear and probably assumed the worst anyway.

A car rumbled in the distance, and she sighed. It was probably her mother's driver climbing the hill. Was it natural to dread seeing your own mother? She didn't know because she had rarely discussed her feelings with anyone. Assuming most women her age had an idyllic relationship with their mothers, Georgie regretted that their relationship was so complicated. Still, it was easier than the non-existent relationship she had with her father. They had only a few stilted conversations since her wedding day, and that was probably a few too many. She stood to watch the sedan pull in front of the house. Her mother quickly emerged, wearing an enormous hat and sunglasses.

"Hello, Mum," Georgie greeted her, walking forward to kiss her cheek.

"Hello, love," her mother said absentmindedly as she directed the driver to carry her luggage inside the house.

"Mum, is there a reason you're wearing that grand hat? You look like you are in disguise or something." Georgie tried to stifle a smile.

"I am wearing this hat and sunglasses for a very good reason. Despite my heritage, I do not want to be out in this hot Sicilian sun." She glanced over at Georgie, wearing her navy sleeveless top and white shorts. "Georgina Anne, you need to take better care of your skin. You're going to look fifty by the time you turn thirty."

"Mum, can you call me Georgie? Every time you say Georgina Anne like that, it makes me feel like I am five years old and in trouble at school."

Her mother took off her sunglasses and squinted at her. "I named you Georgina Anne. I didn't name you Georgie."

"Yes, but that's what I go by. No one calls me Georgina and especially not Georgina Anne. Please, at least can you do that here? I do not want people from the village thinking we're even more haughty than we are."

Her mother sighed, glancing around. "I never fit in here. I was born in this house, raised in this house, and yet, I never once felt I belonged. If I didn't look so much like my mother, I would have sworn I was adopted."

Georgie smiled a little. Putting an arm around her mother's slim shoulders, she ushered her inside just as the driver was exiting. Her mother's quick dismissal of him made Georgie cringe again. Elena was simply unaware of her actions and was going to stand out like a sore thumb in the community that Georgie wanted to embrace. This had been the only place she felt truly like herself. She and her mother were exact opposites.

"Have a seat and I'll get you a glass of lemonade," Georgie offered.

"No, thank you. Too much sugar for me. A glass of water would be lovely."

Georgie tried not to make a face as she walked away. She had made the large jug of lemonade earlier and was proud of her exact replication of her grandmother's signature drink. She poured herself a glass and took both drinks into the well-used living room. *Nonno's* big, comfortable chair was occupied by her mother, who was sitting in it stiffly. For a moment, Georgie saw a glimmer of sadness cross her mother's face, but then just as quickly, she blinked, and the expression was gone.

"Tell me what you have been doing with your time here. You said little on the phone."

Georgie told her about all the arrangements for the *festa*. "It's all come together, and it's a real community effort. I've ordered all the food from Maria, who runs the restaurant up the hill, and some women are coming early to bring linens and help with the decorating. I've also asked one of the teenagers who usually works at the farm to round up some friends and hang some strings of lights. It's going to be a marvelous *festa*."

Her mother sighed audibly. "I cannot believe your grandfather wanted a spectacle after his death."

Georgie frowned. "But it won't be a spectacle. It is going to be a lovely party with people eating, dancing, singing, and chatting. I hope we hear plenty of stories about *Nonno* and *Nonna*."

"What about that farmer? I suppose he'll be here."

Georgie was confused for a minute. "You mean Nico? Mother, he's hardly a farmer. His family owns half of this island! They are the largest exporter in Italy of lemon products. His family is worth billions."

"I do not care about his wealth. But I could hear how angry

you were when you called and told me your grandfather tied you to him for life. It is unexpected, to say the least."

Georgie shrugged. "I know it's difficult to understand. But he wanted things done his own way. He was as stubborn as an ox."

At her mother's silence, Georgie stood and retrieved a box from the table. "Look at what I found in the attic. There are lots of fabulous old photos. I thought we could place a few up on a table at the *festa* for people to enjoy."

She carried the box over to where her mother was sitting, placing it on the coffee table. Elena glanced at her thoughtfully and then carefully took out a handful of photos. She began to look through them, and her expression crumbled. Elena wiped tears from her eyes with a trembling hand. "Oh Georgie," she whispered. "I wish things could have been different."

GEORGIE SAT on the floor next to her mother, and as if she were a small child, she put her head in her mother's lap to comfort her. Georgie let her weep for a while, shocked at the display of emotion. The most emotion she had ever seen her mother show was when she met a renowned author or published a new book herself. At her mother's silence, Georgie finally lifted her head to see Elena's watery smile.

"Do you want to talk about it, Mum?"

Elena looked down, tearing a tissue apart in small pieces with her hands. "I told you I never fit in here. And it's true. I took it out on my parents," she said sadly. "They worked so hard, Georgie. And yet I never helped them around the farm unless I was forced to. I read, I studied, and then I read some more. My sole goal was getting into Oxford. I was obsessed with it all. I'm not even sure why. I had never been there. But I read about it and dreamed about it."

Georgie patted her mother's hand, and she stopped tearing

the tissue, putting the pieces in her lap, seemingly lost in thought. "When I received that scholarship, all my dreams came true. I packed up my one suitcase and would have marched out of here if it wasn't for my parent's insistence that they drive me to the airport in Palermo."

"They surprised me, though. They arranged for us to stay in a hotel for the night. I don't know where they came up with the money. It was so expensive for them. That evening after dinner, they took me to one of Palermo's puppet shows. Even though I was eighteen years old, I must admit it was fun and exciting. Oh, how we laughed together. We had such a grand evening. It was like they were making one last effort to show me a wonderful time before I left. As if they knew."

Georgie stared at her mother. "Knew what?"

"That I would never come back."

"I never asked you about any of this before," Georgie remarked.

"And I wouldn't have told you the truth before now," Elena said softly. "I was too ashamed. By the time you settled in here, you already adored them. I have always known you wouldn't understand. I was just a young girl, Georgie. Once I got on my own in England and met influential people, I let the affluence go to my head. I was embraced by people I never thought I would know. I spent a lot of time and energy focused on what I guess you would call rebranding in today's world. I bought different clothes with the money my parents sent me each month. I styled myself to be just like all my friends. I cut my hair into a trendy style. I did everything I could not to look ethnic, if you know what I mean."

"And then you met Daddy," Georgie filled in.

"Yes, then I met your father. He loved my brain, and he was proud of my work at the college. He encouraged me to continue. Of course, he knew where I was from, but he used to remark casually that most people wouldn't even know I was born and raised in Sicily. I think he meant it as some sort of compliment, but looking back, it made me feel horrible that I just walked away so easily from my heritage."

"You never wanted to come home?"

"This wasn't my home anymore, Georgie! And I was frightened! I thought if I came back, I could lose everything I had built. I argued with *Nonno* on the phone—he didn't understand any of my independence. It was like my childhood all over again, where he tried to tell me what to do. It was always the same fight, that I belonged at home, near family. He insisted I bring your father to Nizza so they could meet him before marrying him. I knew enough to know that would be a disaster, so I told George I preferred a quiet wedding. I didn't tell my parents until afterwards."

Tears welled up in Georgie's eyes. She could almost feel her grandparents' pain. "But you were their only child!"

"Don't you think I knew that? I felt awful. They tried to act happy for me, but I could hear their sadness over the phone. Our calls became less frequent. My mother continued calling, but my father would never come to the phone. We were both so stubborn. I was riddled with guilt, yet I couldn't make the first step toward reconciliation. And so I gave them you."

Georgie looked confused. "I was the olive branch? But why did you wait until I was ten years old? Why didn't you send me sooner?"

A flush rose in her mother's face. "Your father and I argued about it. He didn't want you going at all. The compromise was that you would begin spending holidays here at the age of ten. We reasoned that by that time, all your British upbringing would be ingrained in you."

Georgie's eyes widened. "You really thought it was so awful here? You didn't want me to embrace this part of my culture at all?"

Elena made a small face. "Please understand, Georgie. Now

people travel to Sicily on holiday and post fabulous photos of their trips. Suddenly Sicily is popular, and people are enchanted with the food, the history, the people. But back in the day, there was a stigma that we weren't good enough. That we weren't educated. And deeper, dark stories about what was going on in Sicily. I simply wanted to leave it behind."

Georgie stood now, rubbing her arms in the coolness of the house. "And so, you gave up your parents?"

Elena nodded. "Don't judge me, Georgie. I didn't have the same relationship you did with them. Mamma and I had a better relationship, but Papa and I crossed swords at every opportunity. When I saw and heard him being so gentle and kind to you, I was actually jealous." She gave a bitter laugh. "Can you believe that? Envious of my own child?"

"They loved you," Georgie said softly. "They were proud of you, too. I heard them often talking about you to friends here."

She shrugged. "Maybe they were proud, but they were deeply hurt. In the Italian culture, you stay together. Family is everything. Family is forever. And I left."

"But you came back!" Georgie reminded her gently. "You tried to get the best care for *Nonna* and helped her in the end. And I know you wanted to help *Nonno* more."

Elena looked away, apparently lost in thought. She finally looked at Georgie. "I have spent so much time thinking about the things I didn't like here. Perhaps it's time I realize the best part of my culture. I'm happy you were able to know and love them."

"Family is forever," Georgie said softly.

"Family is forever," Elena repeated. And for the first time in a long time, she gave Georgie a genuine hug.

nine

Georgie smiled widely at an elderly couple doing the *Tarantella*, a traditional Italian folk dance at the *festa*. Everything had turned out exactly as she had pictured it. The tables were covered in colorful Italian linen, and the flowers on the tables were just as bright. People were eating and drinking, and laughter filled the air. Georgie had been busy all night, chatting with the guests, relieved that Nico mostly stayed away from her. He'd arrived, handsome in his khaki pants and cream shirt. Apparently, others thought so, too, as many attractive women approached him from all angles.

Determined not to let it bother her, she turned her attention to the couple on the dance floor. They moved together as one, graceful and in sync, showcasing the familiar dance. Despite their age and the fact that they had been married forever, they still looked deeply in love. That's how her grandparents had been. She had never really seen a love that deep between a man and a woman until she had come to Sicily. She had felt so secure with them because their love had transcended to her.

"They are lovely, aren't they?"

Georgie turned to her mother standing next to her, also

intent on the couple. Since confessing her feelings about the past, Elena was more relaxed and lighter than Georgie had ever witnessed. When Elena came out wearing a dress of *Nonna*'s, with bright red ruffles, Georgie almost fell over in shock. Sharing the same petite frame as *Nonna*, Elena was the only one who could fit into it, yet it was a far stretch from her usual buttoned-up designer attire.

Georgie had selected a floral yellow sundress, and she decided for once not to tame her hair. It floated around her shoulders in a massive cloud. She was pleasantly surprised when her mother didn't even remark on its wildness.

Georgie turned to stare at her mother. "Mum, I was just thinking that *Nonno* and *Nonna* loved me unconditionally."

Elena smiled a little. "Yes, they did, Georgie."

"And they also loved you unconditionally," Georgie added.

Elena turned a startled gaze toward her. "What are you saying?"

Georgie gently wrapped an arm around her mother's slender shoulders. "They always loved you, no matter what, and they knew you loved them, too. I think it's time for you to forgive yourself. You were here for both of them toward the end, and that mattered."

Elena reached up to dab her eyes. "Do you really think so?"

Like their roles had been reversed, it was time for her to comfort her mother. "I do. And it is time to let it go."

Elena nodded. "I'll work on that, Georgie. And I promise that you and I will work on things between us. I've been thinking about it, and I let your father have too much control." She grimaced. "It's almost like I married a man too much like my father."

The music ended, and couples were strolling out to the dance floor under the fairy lights. Her mother suddenly smiled. "This gorgeous night is not the time for such a deep conversation.

Thank you, Georgie. But now we need to enjoy our evening. You should dance and mingle."

"Can I have this dance?"

Georgie turned a startled gaze toward Nico's smiling face. Had he been eavesdropping? Politely, she indicated her mother. "Nico, I would like to introduce my mother, Elena."

Nico smiled charmingly at Elena. "Your mother and I have already been acquainted. We spoke earlier."

Georgie looked uncomfortably from one to the other. She didn't like her mother's sudden innocent expression. "Yes, you go dance, love," Elena remarked casually, as she walked away to greet other guests.

Nico pulled her onto the dance floor and gathered her in his arms. The band was playing a slow Italian ballad. Trying to hold herself stiffly away from Nico, she said, "I apologize if my mother gave you a rough time. I mean, about the will," she rushed to clarify.

"Your mother and I had a delightful conversation. We talked about the will, but she didn't seem upset with me."

Georgie frowned slightly. "Really? Because earlier..."

"Georgie, quit talking."

"But..."

Because she was distracted, Nico easily pulled her in closer. She was forced to nestle her face into his shoulder. "Let's just dance," he said quietly.

Georgie didn't respond. She couldn't if she tried. Despite the countless hours they spent together as teenagers and then young adults, they had never shared a dance. Now she deeply regretted that. She inhaled Nico's subtle spicy cologne in the embrace of his strong, reassuring arms. Everything simply melted away. Time ceased, and she was suddenly at peace.

The music ended and Georgie tried to draw away, but Nico's arms stubbornly held onto her. Another slow ballad began, as the band knew it was getting late and the crowd was in a laid-back mood. The couple continued dancing through three more songs. With her eyes closed, Georgie was in a different world and was startled when the music stopped. She opened her eyes to see the band putting their instruments into their cases. Aware of Nico's arms still around her, she pulled away but instantly met his gaze. Slowly his head descended, blotting out the twinkly lights above their heads. His lips were mere inches from hers, his breath fanning her face. Later, she would admit to herself it was her fault as she leaned in. Their lips met, and though she was expecting an explosion, it was sweeter than she'd imagined. His kiss was gentle, exploring her lips slowly.

Suddenly Georgie came to her senses. They were kissing right there on the dance floor in front of most of the town. Kissing publicly at a celebration such as this was akin to a proposal in Sicily. Despite her desire for the kiss to go on forever, Georgie followed her initial instinct and succumbed to panic. Pushing his chest hard, she stepped back awkwardly. Later, she couldn't recall how she moved or what she tripped over, but she found herself falling. She awkwardly reached out her left hand to break her fall and then came the searing pain.

ten

Georgie woke up in a haze. Moving her arm slightly brought a stabbing pain. It was propped up on a fluffy pillow that her mother had positioned for her. The prior night's events came rushing back like a nightmare. What a moron she was! Having Nico's soft lips on hers was so breathtaking she nearly saw stars. Yet, it was too much for her to take in. Though she desperately wanted the kiss to continue, she became hyper-aware of the crowd, including her mother, for heaven's sake. Their first kiss after all these years shouldn't be in front of a crowd. Besides, over the last several days, he acted like he couldn't stand the sight of her. Now, in front of everyone in town, he was kissing her?

Still, her own clumsy self was her undoing. As soon as she landed, she knew she was injured. A collective gasp had come from the crowd. Nico bent over her, his expression grim. People shouted to stay down, and a local doctor quickly approached. Examining her, he clearly thought her arm was broken. His advice was to keep it elevated that night and put it in a sling until they could get to the hospital in Palermo and have it x-rayed and set. The remaining guests offered to clean up as Nico silently drove Georgie and Elena up to the hill further to the house. He stiffly told her *buonanotte* as she went into the bedroom with her mother, who helped her undress. Beyond fatigued and still a little distressed, Georgie tumbled into bed.

It wasn't going to do her any good to be upset this morning. Still, she wanted to rewind the clock for just ten seconds prior to the kiss. If she hadn't leaned in, none of this would have happened. Now, Georgie had no alternative but to get her arm set if it was broken and return to England with her mother. Earlier, she had thought about staying in Sicily for at least a couple more weeks. She and Nico had to come to some sort of agreement about the management of the farm. They needed to plan how they could work together in the future. The sparks flew between them last night revealed the potent attraction, but the weight of their past hurt and baggage was too much to work through. Her instinct to draw away last night and not to publicly declare her feelings was correct despite the outcome. Sighing, she sat up and swung her legs over the bed, cradling her arm. She grabbed the sling the doctor had made in haste with a dish towel and put it around her neck, gingerly putting her arm in it. It didn't look too swollen, but it hurt a lot. Its shades of purple and green were prominent in some areas. Georgie's stomach rumbled, as last night's food at the *festa* seemed like a long time ago. Once she had something to eat, she would take a pain reliever and see about getting to the hospital.

She walked out to the living room in her short pajama set, and her mother's voice was nearby. Was she talking on the phone? Going out onto the empty porch, Georgie frowned slightly. A delicious aroma wafted by, making Georgie's nose twitch. Her mother never cooked. In fact, she didn't even know *how* to cook.

Walking into the kitchen, cradling her arm protectively, Georgie stopped dead in her tracks. Elena was sitting at the round kitchen table sipping a cup of espresso. Nico was wearing a ridiculous floral apron that was awkwardly tied around him. He turned as he lifted a cast-iron skillet out of the oven.

"*Buongiorno*, Georgie," he said cheerfully. "You're just in time for breakfast!"

~

GEORGIE SPEARED a piece of Nico's delicious tomato, parmigiana, and prosciutto frittata and tried to keep her face impassive. It was like she had stepped into an alternative universe, and it was easier to stay silent.

Nico had served them all a portion of his frittata before sitting down. Also on the table were her favorite wild berries and *cornetto*'s, the Italian version of a croissant. Georgie sat silently. Why was she annoyed to find Nico in her grandparents' kitchen chatting away with her mother after making her favorite breakfast? How could he know this would be her order in a restaurant?

"Georgie, my love, is it very painful?" Elena asked.

Georgie set her fork down and adjusted her arm in the sling. It's okay, Mum. The pills Nico gave me should kick in soon." That Nico knew exactly where to find everything irritated her as well. He had gone to the cabinet near the sink to retrieve the over-the-counter pain reliever that *Nonno* liked to keep next to the juice glasses.

"Do you want more berries?" Nico asked, as he put another helping on his plate.

"Uh, no thank you," Georgie said. With her good hand, she reached up and tried to tame her tangled curls. She probably looked a sight. Today, of all days, was not the time to meet Nico at the breakfast table.

"So, did you just wake up today and decide to come over and cook our breakfast?" Georgie asked bluntly. He gave her an odd look. It was Elena who spoke. "Nico spent the night here last night on the couch. It seemed the best decision since he offered to drive us to Palermo."

"I thought we should all have a good breakfast before we leave," offered Nico. "There will be an orthopedic doctor from Milan waiting when we arrive. If you prefer, we can also go by helicopter. I have one on standby."

Georgie shook her head. "A car is fine. But Nico, you don't have to take me. My mother and I can get a driver."

She gave her mother a speaking look, but the older woman seemed to be purposely avoiding her gaze.

"It's no problem, Georgie," Nico said firmly. "Once you...er... get dressed, we can depart."

Those words seemed to spark Elena into action. She stood and smiled at Georgie. "Let's go get you ready, love. The sooner you get this arm taken care of, the faster you will heal."

Georgie's mother departed the room. This was her chance to convince Nico that they could go alone. He was busy clearing dishes. Realizing it was a lost cause, she stood up too quickly, jostling her arm. The sudden pain made her unsteady, and she might have fallen again if Nico hadn't been there to grasp her.

"*Dio*, you almost fell again," he said, his breath in her ear, sending a tingle down her spine despite the pain. "Let me help you."

She acquiesced to Nico's strong arm as he guided her back to her bedroom. Elena was already there evaluating Georgie's clothes. Nico helped her sit on the bed and stared at her intently for a moment. It was too much this morning to deal with him. Finally, he backed out, closing the door.

Getting dressed and having her mother tend to her needs took longer than Georgie wanted. Her practical mother seemed to sense her mood. "Once you get a cast on your arm, you'll be able to move it more. You won't need as much assistance. Goodness, I haven't dressed you like this since you were five years old."

Georgie bit back the response that her mother rarely dressed her; it was usually her nanny. It wasn't worth spoiling their truce, and if her mother wanted to fuss over her now, so be it. Elena packed a suitcase for her. Georgie told her she might as well pack everything, since now they would return to England. Her mother was strangely silent.

It took a while, but finally Georgie, now exhausted, found herself sitting in the back of Nico's luxury black SUV, not his usual Jeep. Nico had put two pillows on the seat and adjusted her arm on it. Elena climbed into the passenger seat as if she and Nico were the best of friends. Nico was an excellent driver, and soon, Georgie stopped fighting her body's desire for sleep, slowly closing her eyes to slip into a quiet slumber.

NICO TRIED to steady his thoughts as he drove quickly and skillfully toward Palermo. Traffic was getting heavier, and he was forced to concentrate. Elena chatted most of the way, but he was having a difficult time focusing on what she was saying, except that she planned to return to England once Georgie was treated. Apparently, she needed to get back to plan for the next term.

After Georgie fell asleep, he explained to Elena that he called Meara's husband, Doctor Alessandro Amato, earlier that morning. Nico asked for one of the best orthopedic surgeons to meet them at Palermo's hospital. The doctor was flying in from Milan and would work out privileges to treat Georgie in Palermo. Unfortunately, Nico had to call his sister-in-law, Kate, to get Meara's number to put the plan into action. Meara asked several questions, which Nico answered as briefly as possible. She seemed to sense he was in no mood to linger and with a sigh, put Alec on the phone. Soon, Alec had arranged for Doctor Maloberti to call him.

Nico glanced into his rearview mirror and smiled. Georgie's

head was lolled back against the expensive leather, her mouth slightly ajar. A small snore escaped. He was pleased she was able to sleep. It worried him this morning how pale she was, and he knew she was in more pain than she let on. She hadn't even eaten very much of the breakfast he knew she loved.

Knowing it was irrational, he still kicked himself for not breaking her fall last night. It felt like everything had happened in slow motion. Leaning in to kiss her had been impulsive, and yet the tug to do was so strong there was no way he could stop himself. Focused solely on feeling her lips on his again, he had almost been in a daze when she pulled back and then tripped over a small child's toy that somehow made it to the dance floor. At first, he thought she hit her head because of her confused expression. But then when he saw the swelling begin in her arm, he knew it was broken. The doctor who was present advised ice and elevation, but Nico still fought off the desire to put her in his car and get her to the hospital immediately. It was only after conferring with the doctor that he realized that was probably not the best course of action, since they needed the swelling to go down before setting it.

It had been all he could do to wait until morning. In fact, he had slept on the couch just in case Georgie or Elena needed him. The crick in his neck was a reminder of his own weakness. He was happy he had a change of clothes in his car, though, even if it was only jeans and a T-shirt.

Georgie's mixed signals the night before puzzled him. At first, he felt her lean into his kiss enthusiastically. But the look on her face when she pulled away was a mixture of horror and panic. It had made his heart sink. His resolve now was to get her medical treatment, put her on an airplane and consult with his oldest brother on how to best manage this co-ownership with her. Marco would know what to do.

A quick glance in the rearview mirror at Georgie startled him. Her deep blue eyes were staring back at him. How long had she been awake? He quickly turned his gaze away and listened to what Elena was saying.

"Honestly, Georgie has always been clumsy. Don't blame yourself, Nico."

"Mum, please. No one blames Nico. I simply tripped," Georgie insisted from the backseat.

Elena nodded. "That is what I am trying to convey to him, love. Remember the time you tried sliding down the banister and broke your leg? Or the time you insisted our chef teach you how to cook and you cut yourself badly?" She turned to look at Nico. "She had to have so many stitches they called in a plastic surgeon," she confided. "You can hardly notice them on her hand."

"Mum, perhaps we can talk about something else!"

Her mother seemed nonplused. "That's honestly why I am still a little nervous about her being a…"

"MUM!" Georgie interrupted, her voice rising. "Please!"

Nico couldn't bite back his smile. "I find this fascinating," he remarked, giving her a quick glance in the mirror.

"You would," Georgie remarked bitterly.

He instantly regretted teasing her. "*Mi dispiace*, Georgie, I know this isn't what you needed right now to happen. I'm confident that the doctor Alec found is going to get your arm fixed, and it will heal soon."

Georgie looked out the window, a small frown on her face. Finally, she spoke softly. "And then I'll return to London and put it all behind me."

Nico stared straight ahead at the road, contemplating her statement. Was it possible for her to put everything behind her? He realized it wouldn't be that simple for him. Perhaps that's why he suddenly felt so depressed.

eleven

G eorgie blinked her eyes open. Her throat was so dry she felt like she couldn't swallow. Glancing quickly around, she couldn't help but notice the starkness of the white walls that surrounded her. She adjusted her arm and felt a dull ache. An I.V. bottle was filtering some kind of medicine into her, and a monitor was blinking numbers she couldn't quite focus on.

Turning her head, she saw Nico's profile. Curled up in a large leather chair, wearing worn jeans and a faded T-shirt, he was dead to the world. She took a minute to admire him, loving the strong cheekbones and the long eyelashes that rested on them. His black wavy hair was now untidily spilling over his ears. When sleeping, he looked so much younger, almost like the Nico of her youth. Once he woke, he would become the serious Nico, the one that seemed so unfamiliar to her. It didn't matter anyway, since soon she would be in England and out of his life.

Trying to swallow her dry throat, she reached for the water bottle that was on the tray near her bed. Overshooting it, she knocked it off the tray, and it fell to the ground with a loud thunk. Nico sat up as if he had been shot. Disoriented, he glanced around the room before looking down and seeing the

81

bottle. Picking it up, he placed it back on the tray. It was then his gaze finally met Georgie's.

"You're awake," he said softly, stating the obvious. Pushing his hair back impatiently, he leaned over her. Extending his arm above her head, he rested his hand on the bed. His eyes searched her face. "How do you feel?"

Georgie attempted to speak, but her throat was making it difficult. She tried clearing it and pointed to the bottle.

"*Dio*, you need water, don't you?" Nico exclaimed. "*Uno momento*. Let me get you a clean bottle."

He was back in a minute, holding a straw from a water bottle up to her mouth. She drank greedily and then nodded for him to withdraw it. It was a strangely intimate gesture, and she averted her eyes from his intense gaze.

"Thank you," she whispered. "Where's my mother?"

"She went back to the hotel to rest," he told her. Glancing at his watch, he continued, "It's after five o'clock in the morning, Georgie. You've been out ever since the doctor operated. You came to for a few minutes but then just passed right back out. The doctor said everything went well, though."

It all flooded back to Georgie then. She remembered meeting Doctor Malberto. In his mid-thirties, he was remarkably handsome and had been charming to her. He had examined Georgie's arm and ordered an x-ray. Nico had frowned at him, but then proceeded to ask numerous questions. After reviewing the x-ray, Doctor Malberto was firm that surgery was required to help piece together her bones and he probably needed to use a couple screws and a small plate. The hospital was busy, and they waited for several hours before he could operate.

She glanced down at the navy-blue cast on her arm that went past her elbow. At least it was fixed.

"How long do I have to stay here?" Georgie asked.

"I think you can probably leave today. It was so late by the time Doctor Malberto could operate. It just seemed a good decision to let you spend the night."

Georgie nodded slowly. "Has my mother made our flight arrangements?"

Nico didn't look at her. He was busy at the curtains, drawing them back. "It's a beautiful sunrise," he drawled, his tone sounding guarded.

"Nico, what aren't you telling me? Was there something else wrong?"

"No, no, Georgie, you're fine. The doctor is pleased, and he's already departed for Milan. He gave instructions to the head of orthopedics here to check on you before releasing you."

"That was nice of Marco to use his plane to fly him down."

Nico nodded, still staring outside.

Georgie shifted uncomfortably. "And I'm sorry, Nico. I never thanked you. It was thoughtful of you to find a doctor who could see me so quickly, and someone we knew we could trust, especially since I needed surgery." Nico again inclined his head but was avoiding looking at her.

"So, back to traveling. Do you know if my mother wants to leave today?"

Nico finally turned and stared at her. "Yes, she does. She has a flight scheduled for ten this morning."

Georgie's eyes widened. "This morning?" She tried to sit up straighter, pushing the mattress with her uninjured hand. "We should call for the nurse. I better start asking about getting released and get this stuff out of me," she said, pointing to the I.V. bag and the monitor. "That doesn't leave me much time."

"Georgie, you're not going with her," he remarked calmly.

She looked at him, confused. "I'm not? Why not?"

"Because you're going to stay here with me."

∼

AS NICO DROVE, Georgie faced the window, focusing on the passing scenery, determined to stop gazing at him. If she continued, she would be helpless against admiring his strong, tan arms below the rolled-up sleeves of his light blue shirt. The large silver watch he wore glinted in the sunlight. He had left the hospital for a short time and returned, dressed more formally in khaki pants with a button-down shirt. He looked like he had showered as well, his hair tamed.

Elena had visited while he was gone, explaining apologetically that she really needed to return to England. Georgie offered to go with her on a later flight, but her mother cautioned that she would need a little extra care for a few days. "At least it's your left arm," she said cheerfully. "You can do the, uh, personal things for yourself. But darling, you really need to rest for several days and go for your follow-up visit at the hospital."

Georgie had learned that while she was in the operating room, Nico had managed to persuade Elena that his villa in Taormina was the ideal place for Georgie's recovery. Elena assured her that Nico's housekeeper could provide assistance for anything she might require. Georgie was annoyed by the fact that they hatched this plan without consulting her. When Nico returned, he was met with her icy disdain.

It was admittedly hard to keep up her irritation as she and Nico waited for her discharge, with nurses checking her vitals, the doctor evaluating her arm and providing discharge orders. Nico had been more than helpful, going to the pharmacy to pick up her medication, and listening to everything the doctor advised.

Now, as she sat in the car, she adjusted her arm in its sling, gingerly moving it and absorbing the newfound weight.

"Are you still angry with me?"

Georgie turned to finally face him. "I just don't understand how you and my mother cooked up this plan at a time when I couldn't even object."

He glanced at her, but his sunglasses obscured his eyes. She couldn't help but frown at the sly smirk on his face.

"Georgie, there was no cooking up anything. This was not the grand conspiracy you think it is. Your mother needed to go back to England, and well, I feel at fault for the whole thing. The least I can do is let you heal at my home."

"I tripped over a toy, Nico. It was not your fault," Georgie said. She prayed he wouldn't bring up their kiss. It would be so humiliating to admit she acted like a naïve fifteen-year-old receiving her first kiss.

"Regardless, I feel responsible. Let me at least help you until you return to England."

Georgie frowned irrationally at his assumption that she would just go back home after her arm healed, despite the fact that it was what she intended. "What if I want to stay in Sicily?" she grumbled.

He glanced quickly at her. "You are considering that?"

She shrugged but remained silent, wallowing in her irrational annoyance. It was difficult to shake this mood.

The car climbed the hill, and as it swept around a bend, the Ionian Sea came into view. Nico punched a code into a gate, and it swung open so they could ascend the winding road. Finally, at the last turn, they came upon a white villa standing majestically at the top of the hill. What Georgie noticed more than the expansive house, however, was the abundant plants and flowers. A garden surrounded the front entrance.

"Oh, Nico!" she whispered. "It's beautiful."

He took off his sunglasses, throwing them on the dash, and turned to stare at her, his face impassive.

"Welcome to my home, Georgie."

As he helped her out of the car, she was able to glance around even more. She inhaled the sweet fragrance of flowers mingled with the salty sea air. Smiling, she reached up to wrestle her hair out of her eyes as a gentle breeze blew. "Did you plant all this or just design it?" she asked, already knowing the answer.

"I planted every piece," he acknowledged, taking her uninjured arm to steady her while they walked up the stone path. "I didn't have a plan, but I knew what I wanted. It's difficult to explain."

"I know what you mean," Georgie said. "I remember how you used to dream about having a house on a hill overlooking the sea. And how you wanted it surrounded by flowers that made the air smell like perfume and plants that fed the soil. And you wanted a kitchen garden off the back, where you could grow your own vegetables and herbs. And, of course, you would have lemon and olive trees."

He stopped walking to turn and stare incredulously at her. "You remember that?"

She smiled a little without answering. It would mean admitting that she committed everything he used to dream about to memory.

Through the extra-wide mahogany front door was a black-and-white tile floor, and a grand staircase loomed to the right. In front of them stood a round mahogany table adorned with a massive vase overflowing with vibrant, fresh flowers.

"I'll show you to your room," Nico said. "You must be tired. It's been a long day."

Slowly, Georgie climbed the curved staircase and followed him to a room to the right. He opened the French doors, and she sighed at the luxurious surroundings.

"It's beautiful, Nico." Walking over to the floor-to-ceiling windows that overlooked the sea, she admired the view. "Just like you wanted."

She didn't dare turn around, but he must have been staring at her because he stayed silent. Finally, he spoke, and his voice was rough. "I'll have someone bring up your bag. And I'll ask Angelina to bring you some dinner on a tray."

She opened her mouth to argue. Couldn't they at least eat dinner together? But suddenly, the remote Nico was back. In addition, her weariness began to creep in, and the bed appeared increasingly tempting.

She turned to him. "Thank you," she said simply. He inclined his head politely and paused as if he was going to say something else but didn't. Abruptly, he headed out the door, closing it with a firm click.

Georgie sunk into the comfortable chair near the French doors that led to a balcony. How did her world get so out of control? What had transpired to get her to Nico's villa, and why was she here? Nothing made sense anymore. She didn't sit with her thoughts for long. Soon, Angelina stuck her head around the door. Her silver hair was cut short, her dark eyes were compassionate. She helped Georgie into her short jammies, brought her a tray of delicious food, and tsk tsked at her injury. Angelina talked the entire time in Italian, never stopping to take a breath. Georgie only smiled. It was like having a nanny as an adult, and the attention was rather nice.

Sinking into the comfortable bed, she went over the day. The villa was just as Nico had described to her many years ago. The home of his dreams. His description had been so vivid, she had seen it in her own dreams. But she wasn't part of his life, and the villa wasn't something they built together. Life had taken them on twists and turns, and now fate was poking her nose into things. Georgie sighed and closed her eyes. She'd worry about it all tomorrow.

twelve

Georgie woke to a dull ache in her arm. Completely disoriented, she blinked for a moment, trying to remember where she was. Grimacing in pain, she glanced over to see Nico sitting in the chair by the balcony. A small reading lamp cast a faint glow on his serious, handsome face. As if he sensed her attention, he looked up and held her gaze. The moment passed quickly, though, as he stood and walked over to her. Putting one arm on the headboard of the bed, tender concern was evident in his eyes.

"George, are you in pain?"

She nodded, having trouble forming words. He looked...well, almost like the old Nico.

He brushed the strands away from her face gently, before putting a pillow behind her and gently propped her up. He opened a bottle, handing her a pill, which she took with the glass of water he then provided. Gratefully, she drank through the straw.

He gingerly sat on the end of the bed, as far as he could from her. She moved her legs slightly to give him more room. With her arm propped up on pillows, it was difficult to move around too much.

"What time is it?" she asked for something to say.

He glanced at his watch. "Just after three."

She looked at him, surprised. "You've been up all night?"

"When I picked up your prescription, the pharmacist told me the pain medication would wear off in the middle of the night. You went to sleep before I had a chance to tell you that. You slept longer than I thought. I'm glad, though."

Georgie picked at a thread on the comforter with her right hand, avoiding his gaze. "That was nice of you, Nico. You could have just left me a pill by the bed."

"I'm occasionally a nice person," he commented, grinning a little, his deep dimples appearing.

She raised her head sharply to stare at him. "Nico, you've always been a nice person."

He stayed silent, his gaze intent. Finally, he stood. "Not always, but that's a discussion for another time. You should get some sleep. And so should I. You probably won't need your next pill until about nine. I'll leave it here for you. But just remember to not take it before then."

He walked toward the door before turning. "Do you need anything before I go?"

Swallowing hard, she bit back her desire to plead, "Don't go!" How could she tell him that she wished with all her heart he would simply lay down next to her? Just to feel his comforting presence would go a long way in erasing the sudden loneliness she felt. Instead, she shook her head and settled back against the pillow.

He stood looking at her before walking back toward her. He leaned over her again, and she automatically closed her eyes. Disappointment overcame her when she felt his cool lips on her forehead. Exhausted, the last thing she remembered before she dozed off was that he had called her George.

NICO WALKED around his property with a spade. Giovanni, his trusted gardener, hurried alongside him. While Nico was responsible for planting his expansive gardens, he counted on Giovanni to tend to them full-time. Nico wasn't always at the villa, but he insisted things remain well cared for.

Giovanni pointed out some transplanted shrubs he had been nursing. With one ear, Nico half-listened to the gardener's musings about how the plants were adapting to their new environment. It suddenly dawned on him that he just mindlessly nodded in agreement to whatever Giovanni had asked. The older man was now walking back toward the toolshed.

The events of the last few days were playing havoc with Nico's mind as he tried to make sense of his jumbled emotions. He had insisted to Elena that she could return to England, and he would take Georgie to his villa. While it was not the grand conspiracy that Georgie thought, it still was premeditated on his part. Skillfully, he nudged her mother into leaving, yearning to have Georgie at his home and all to himself. While rationally he knew it was only a broken arm, her injury rocked him. It was during her surgery that he began making plans. Fate was trying to tell them something, and he was going to seize this opportunity.

Suddenly, the past hurts didn't seem so significant, and it became clear he would always regret not giving their relationship a chance. Now it was time to persuade her, and that might take some doing. Yesterday had been more difficult than he thought. Dressed in her simple jeans and top, her hair disheveled, she resembled his George once more. All he wanted to do was gather her in his arms and tell her things could work out between them. In fact, he was having a rough time keeping his hands off her. Last night, he desperately wanted to stay with her, just to feel the warmth of her body next to his and reassure her that she wasn't alone. He wanted to hear her sweet voice as he drifted off to sleep. Instead, he had gone to bed feeling the intense loneliness that he was now used to.

Lying awake for the few hours that remained of the night, he finally decided the only way to move forward was to strip off the cool exterior he had erected. Georgie needed to see the real him again and the feelings she'd awakened. It meant getting hurt all over again. But if he wasn't willing to try, then why had he even brought her to the villa?

At the balcony outside her window, she stood in her short jammies, a long white robe billowing around her. Her hair was a blonde cloud around her shoulders. He watched her grab it with one hand and pull it impatiently back. That one movement was signature Georgie, and he grinned up at her.

She raised a tentative hand, and he saw her smile slightly. They stood like that for a minute before he abruptly threw the spade down and walked closer to her, never breaking his gaze from hers. "*Buongiorno*," he called, grinning up at her. "You're finally awake."

"Is it still morning, or did I sleep right through it?"

"It's almost eleven, definitely still morning." His smile turned to concern. "Did you wake up in pain? Have you taken your pill?"

She shook her head. "They make me so sleepy. I was hoping I could take something a bit less strong, just to take the edge off."

"I don't want you in pain, Georgie."

"Let me just try! If it gets worse, I'll take them. But I'm desperate to get dressed and have a look around. Your garden is so gorgeous, Nico. Well done!"

He smiled proudly. For a long time, he imagined what Georgie would say if she saw his home, which meant so much to him. While he owned other residences, this one was his home.

"I'll send Angelina up to help you get dressed, and she'll

bring you some ibuprofen. Then we can have lunch or breakfast, in your case, and I'll show you around."

"Okay!" she agreed happily and turned to go into her room. Spinning around, her smile grew. "I can't wait, Nico!"

He stared at the empty balcony for a moment, caught off guard by her girlish enthusiasm. At the same time, the wall he had so carefully built to shield Georgie from breaking his heart yet again crumbled.

<h1 style="text-align:center">*thirteen*</h1>

Georgie dove into her *panino*, chewing with enthusiasm. They were sitting outside on his covered *giardino*. Though the sun was growing warm, the shade felt lovely, and the breeze off the sea was refreshing. She was decidedly hungry, and lunch was delicious. Even more pleasant was Nico's mood. Before lunch, he had given her an extensive tour of his home. To say she was impressed at his attention to detail was an understatement. Starting with her own room, she luxuriated in the multi-head shower and marble vanity. The expansive walk-in closet, with built-ins would be a pleasure to use, but it was laughable currently with her little suitcase sitting in its center. Angelina had hung up her small array of clothes.

There had been more bedrooms to explore, but he had breezed past his, only opening the door to see a massive suite, its decor in neutral tones. Downstairs was a home theater, a state-of-the-art gym, a spacious wine cellar, and a study that had more books in it than she could ever read. She marveled at the two different dining rooms, one that could seat twenty-five and a smaller, more intimate one, with a long, narrow glass fire pit running along the side. Though she rarely cooked, the modern kitchen almost made her want to, as she ran her hand over the Italian marble and stainless-steel appliances. Her favorite aspect was the house's design, which seamlessly opened to the outdoors. Sliding walls revealed comfortable, expansive seating areas that overlooked the lush garden.

While eating, they had kept their conversation general, talking about Taormina and the places they could visit while she recuperated. Nico was talkative, telling her funny stories about his business travels as well. Full now, she put what was left of her *panino* down on her plate and wiped her hand with her napkin. "Nico, I had no idea you managed so much for the company. And at the same time, you've completed all these advanced degrees. I don't know how you did it all."

He shrugged, looking almost embarrassed. "If it's something you're passionate about, it doesn't feel like work. I loved learning everything. And it gave me...I guess confidence that I also knew so much already. It felt almost liberating for the first time to find other people who also were interested in the same things I was. My family never understood. Except *Zio* Angelo, and when he died, there was only..."

"*Nonno*," she said softly.

He smiled, covering her hand. "*Nonno*. He understood because the land meant everything to him."

Despite the tingles going up her spine, she stared at him, her expression serious. "Nico, I want to apologize. I have been selfish and only thought about my grief. I told you about his death so carelessly. I'm sorry I wasn't more compassionate."

"I understood. He was your grandfather, Georgie."

"But..."

Nico interrupted her. "I suggest we call a truce about it and agree we both loved him dearly. That's all that matters now."

This was all so confusing. "Nico..."

His hand left hers to brush a strand of her hair behind her ear. He leaned forward intently. "What if we were to call a truce about everything? Imagine if we just waved the past goodbye and started over?"

"I don't think we can do that," she said cautiously. "It's our past. It's a part of us. But what are you saying? Start over? You and me?"

He was intently staring at her. "Yes."

As he stood, his chair scraped on the stone patio. Glancing around, he stretched an arm out to her. "But this is much too heavy of a conversation right now. It's getting warm, and you look tired, Georgie. Why don't we go inside? Let's take today and tomorrow easy, and then we'll do a little sightseeing. First, you need to rest."

Georgie frowned. They had just been getting somewhere when he retreated again. But Nico was as stubborn as her grandfather had been. He had no intention of continuing their conversation. She stood and took the hand he was offering her. She wouldn't push him now, but he would have to return to this topic. Even if he didn't want to.

NICO SAT by Georgie as she slept on the enormous white sofa, a book resting on her abdomen. She had insisted she wanted to read and not sleep. Earlier, he moved a table over with a pillow, and her arm was cradled there. It was terrible that she had broken it. If he could reverse time, he would, even if it meant that they wouldn't be together now.

The earlier truce idea had sprung from his mouth before he could stop it. She had looked so vulnerable at lunch that he realized he didn't want to inadvertently hurt her by keeping a cool mask. Even if that mask was still a habit he had formed to protect his own heart. Today was a new day, and he was going to show his true self to Georgie again. Time would soon tell what she was feeling. He thought he had seen the answer so many times in her eyes. It seemed that she generally still cared for him, but some of that emotion could just be sweet memories from their past. Nico frowned. Perhaps he should slow down until he got some sign from her.

"What are you frowning about?"

Nico startled, and Georgie struggled to sit up, pushing her hair out of her face in her regular sweep. "I'm sorry I fell asleep. I didn't mean to."

He decided to ignore her question. "Are you in any pain?"

"Just a little. It's manageable."

"You should take the pain pills. I'll go get them."

She shook her head. "No, I'm going to ride it out." She glanced at her watch. "I can take that ibuprofen again in an hour or so. I don't like the way those pain meds make me feel."

"If you're sure," he said doubtfully.

"Positive," she said, adjusting herself to a better sitting position.

"Is there anything you need?"

She looked with raised eyebrows. "Remember that truce we called? Well, it's going to extend to my arm, too. Nico, you have to stop fussing around me like an Italian mother." She gave a small laugh. "My Italian mother doesn't even fuss like that."

He grinned a little sheepishly. "I just want you to be comfortable."

"I'll tell you when I'm not," Georgie said firmly.

She indicated the laptop he pushed aside earlier when he couldn't concentrate. "What are you working on?"

He grimaced. "Just reports for Marco. So much paperwork. It's why I asked to retreat from some of my responsibilities for Oro Industries."

"You're not working for the company as much?"

"I am working in a limited capacity. Both Stefano and I want to take a step back, but we understood Marco needed us for a while until he adjusted to being CEO. He encouraged me to pursue my studies, though. While I did so, Marco was forced to find someone to take on most of my responsibilities. Now I'm carving out a new role where I'm more of an adviser. It's just going to take time, but it will be better in the long run."

"I'm glad you're happy, Nico. I know you never wanted to be surrounded by paperwork."

"What about you, Georgie? I haven't wanted to ask because I thought that you were just married and..." He broke off uncomfortably.

"Wiling away my days? Lunching or having garden parties?"

Nico felt embarrassment rise. "Well, no. But I don't know what you're doing. Do you have a job?"

"Yes, I definitely have a job," she said slowly.

"I'm sorry. I didn't mean to imply anything. Tell me what you do."

He watched as the color rose in her face. She looked almost uncomfortable. What did she do for a living?

"You're not going to like it. That's why I haven't mentioned it. And I swore my family to secrecy."

He sat forward, his mind racing, his expression suddenly grim. He leaned his arms on his knees. "Tell me, George."

She took a deep breath. "I fly for a living."

He looked confused, and she continued. "I am a pilot, Nico. I work for a medical transport company, and I fly medical crews all over the United Kingdom and sometimes beyond. We pick up organs for transplants, or I fly doctors to certain places where no transplant teams exist."

He felt the color drain from his face. "But, Georgie, you're so..."

She glared at him. "Clumsy? Klutzy? Yes, I know Nico. But in the air, I am not. I am a skilled pilot!"

He shook his head, trying to clear his thoughts. "How? When?"

She seemed to be deliberately avoiding looking at him, intently examining her cast. She finally looked up at him.

"I started taking lessons after...after you and I broke off. A friend's father was an instructor and took me up in his plane, and I was hooked. Flying made me so happy. I felt free and wonderful. I kept it a secret from my parents, and I earned my private pilot's license by the time I graduated!"

"So, then you got a job as a pilot?"

She shook her head. "No, it has been a very long road to get where I am. I made the unfortunate decision to tell my parents that's what I wanted to do after university. We had such a row that I withdrew from the idea. They told me to find a 'respectable job,' as they called it. So I did and I was miserable."

At his silence, she continued. "I felt like a failure, and I came to Sicily to see if I could find my passion. I thought about you and how you knew exactly what you wanted to do. That drove me to decide to see you. I just wanted to speak to you and see..." She broke off.

"What did you want to see, George?" he asked softly.

She raised her dark blue eyes to his. "I remembered... how you always seemed to help me figure things out. I thought maybe we could reconnect. But then you weren't home, and I realized how ridiculous the entire plan was. How you weren't sitting at home waiting for me! I returned to England, and I realized aside from Sicily, the happiest I'd ever been was in the air. It's like you were talking about earlier—finding something you love doesn't feel like work! I enrolled in an intensive flight school from there and began flying as many hours as I could."

"And then you got a job as a pilot?"

"Well, no." She looked uncomfortable. "You see, I still had to keep it a secret."

"From your parents."

"Yes. And from my fiancé."

Her face was flushed, and she looked uncomfortable. He

longed to go sit down next to her on the couch and put his arms around her but knew it was too much, too soon. He decided to change course.

"Georgie, you don't have to continue. I… well, I'm grateful that you are telling me finally about your world. Why didn't you think I would like it?

She shrugged. "No one else has really supported the idea."

"I'm not like anyone else," he said softly. "While I am still getting used to the idea, if it's what you love, then who am I to tell you not to do it?" Realizing he just inadvertently asked her about his status in her life, he abruptly changed the subject. "What do you say we go for a swim?"

"Uh, Nico, have you noticed anything? Like maybe a cast on my arm?"

He grinned. "A modified swim. You can still sit on the stairs of the pool, or if you are feeling bold, we can try to tie a plastic bag over it and you can come in the water."

"I don't think I'm quite that daring today," Georgie said slowly. "But I'd love to see the pool and maybe just dangle my legs in a little."

"*Perfetto!*" he said. "I'll meet you in the garden in fifteen minutes."

"Make it twenty," Georgie said. "It's going to take me a few minutes to figure out how to get my bikini on."

Nico swallowed hard. Perhaps this had not been such a good idea. "I'll send Angelina up."

fourteen

Georgie relaxed in the shade, marveling at the size of Nico's saltwater pool that was cleverly concealed on the edge of his property. Below it was a breathtaking view of the sea. Admittedly, she was also appreciating the view of Nico, who was swimming laps, fluid and relaxed and not displaying any kind of exertion.

When he had taken his shirt off to reveal that bronze chest, she had tried to look away but was riveted. Holy God, he looked amazing. Of course, she knew he would. She hadn't seen his body since he was a teenager, but he was definitely a man now, and there was no comparison.

His call for a truce at lunch had surprised her but immediately delighted her. In fact, his mood seemed to have improved drastically since they arrived at his home. What had changed? Perhaps it was just being content in the home he obviously cherished.

"Aren't you going to come in?"

Startled, she stared at Nico as he treaded water, his hair slicked back, his black eyes lively. He always loved the water when they'd taken all their trips to the beach over the years.

"Arm, remember?"

He grinned, his dimples edged in his cheeks. He pointed. "Stairs, remember? Why don't you at least come sit on them? I can put that plastic pillow over there. You can rest your arm on it, but at least you would be in the pool. It's hot, even in the shade!"

She bit back her retort that it was nice and cool inside the house. This had been his idea, and she had gone along with it because she craved being near him. Pointing at her white thigh-high cover-up that she donned over her bikini, she said, "I'll get my cover-up wet."

"Take it off. I'll get out and help you."

Before she could respond, he was heaving himself out of the pool and jumping to his feet. Extending a wet hand, he tugged her out of her chair, leading her over to the stairs. He eyed her for a moment, taking in that her uninjured arm was captured in the coverup's sleeve. "Let me hold your sleeve and you can maneuver your arm out and then I'll lift it off."

"Sure," Georgie responded automatically, before suddenly, she remembered what she was wearing underneath.

"Uh, wait a moment," she blurted.

"Georgie, I've seen a woman in a bikini before," he stated matter-of-factly, misinterpreting her hesitation. "In fact, I've seen a lot of you, if you recall."

She her face flushing. "Well, yes, that was a long time ago. I just need to take something off," she said uncomfortably.

He was staring at her, clearly confused. She turned a little away from him and awkwardly pulled out a long chain and pulled it over her head. As bad luck would have it, her hair tangled with it.

"Wait, wait! It's caught. Let me help," Nico offered.

She waited as he untangled the chain, and she was able to pull it over her head. Turning back toward him, she held the chain and its contents in her covered hand.

"What's on the chain, Georgie?" he asked quietly.

"Nothing. It's just valuable, and I didn't want it to get wet," she quickly explained.

"Open your hand."

Staring at him for a minute, she felt the blood drain from her face. He would think she was so ridiculous, and she would be mortified. Without a choice, she slowly uncurled her fingers to reveal a long gold chain and a small ring.

His startled gaze came up to meet hers. A dark frown soon replaced it.

"Georgie, is that...?"

"Your promise ring? It is. Go on. Have a laugh."

SITTING IN HER ROOM, Georgie gazed longingly at the balcony, imagining the fresh breeze and the stunning view it offered. She desperately wanted to go out on it, but Nico would spot her. He was in the garden, chopping and wielding his spade like he was fighting demons. If she leaned closer toward the window, she could see him, wearing an old pair of shorts, his torso still bare.

After the discovery of the promise ring, she had simply turned and walked into the house rather than face his expression. He hadn't followed her, and she purposely did not turn around. Now she glanced over at the table where she carelessly dropped the chain and ring. How could she ever admit to him that she always wore it on her right hand and had done so every day of her life except when she was engaged? Even though Benjamin had no idea of its context, she felt guilty and banished it to her jewelry box. After her almost wedding, she returned it to her finger willingly. She couldn't explain the comfort it brought her. Knowing it was silly, she wanted no one to know, especially Nico.

Nico gave her the ring the night in Palermo before she left for university. They had been sitting on stone benches near *I Quattro Canti*—the Four Corners. It was a part of Palermo she loved. As the streets intersected, the buildings' corners were designed in baroque facades featuring intricate statues and fountains. Georgie told Nico she could stare at them forever and still not take in every feature. It was also a popular place for musicians since the acoustics were fantastic. They sat there, captivated by the soft musician's voice singing "What a Wonderful World." While they sat on the bench, Nico kissed her in such a way that it made her believe that the world was truly wonderful. He finally drew away and handed her a small box. In it was a small rose gold band with a garnet and sapphire—their birthstones—inlaid in it. At first, she withdrew, worried that he was proposing. Despite being head over heels in love with him, she knew they were too young to be engaged. Sensing her panic, he reassured her it was only a promise ring. That it was his solemn promise that no matter what happened, he would always have a place in his heart for her. Georgie was deeply touched and swept away by it all and promised the same. It was easy to also promise to always be honest with him. He had consented also to do so.

They sat on the bench for hours, her head on his shoulder. And that night in their hotel room, she had begged him to make love to her. Only he had resisted, telling her that he could never look at her grandfather again if he broke his own promise to him.

Georgie had gotten on the plane, wearing his ring, a mass of emotions. When she arrived in England, she switched it to her right hand to avoid any questions from her parents. And when her mother's eagle eye spotted it, Georgie gave her practiced reply, "This? Just a cheap piece of jewelry I bought off a street vendor. I thought it was kind of pretty." It seemed to do the trick, and she continued to wear it on her right hand until she had traveled to Sicily following the death of her grandfather. She had glanced down at it prior to meeting with Nico and had realized how absurd she would look wearing it. Panicked, she took it off and placed it in her make-up bag—until this morning. She had woken up in his home, her mind still swirling with the memories of the tender gaze he had given her the night before. Feeling sentimental, she had fastened it on a long chain, knowing he wouldn't see it under her crew neck shirt. It made her feel warm and hopeful, despite her incredible uncertainty about any kind of relationship with Nico.

A knock on the door startled her from her memories. She glanced outside and didn't see Nico. Oh God, was he going to force a conversation? How was she going to explain she was still wearing his ring a decade after he gave it to her? Perhaps in a way, she rationalized, it was time. Lay all their cards on the table. Her heart sped up, only to drop to her feet when Angelina poked her head in the doorway.

"*Signore* Nico asked me to come up and help you dress. I have made an *aperitivo* for the two of you in the *giardino*."

Georgie nodded, swallowing her own apprehension. Apparently, it *was* time they talked.

fifteen

"Come sit down, Georgie," Nico called, as he stood near the outside table, looking handsome in his black jeans and chocolate brown polo. She looked her best in her favorite yellow floral sundress. She had taken a long shower, and Angelina had helped her dry her hair so her curls were smooth and not frizzy. A little makeup to do battle, and she was ready.

The tremendous amount of flowers made her smile. A giant trellis over the seating area featured climbing lavender wisteria, and multi-colored Italian pots overflowing with flowers dotted the stonework. There were plants and flowers everywhere, and she took a deep breath of the jasmine that was closest to her. She sat on the comfortable furniture and voiced her thoughts. "It's gorgeous out here, Nico. Everyplace in your home is so lovely."

He poured her a glass of crisp pinot grigio and inclined his head at her words. Sitting, he leaned forward, his elbows on the table, his hands under his chin. Staring at her, his expression remained neutral.

On the table, was a wooden tray overflowing with a wide variety of breads, Italian meats, cheeses, and olives. It had been a long time since lunch. Trying to appear relaxed, she popped an olive in her mouth and chewed.

"Shall we talk about the ring?"

Georgie met Nico's direct gaze while she continued to chew. He always got right to the point, didn't he? Swallowing, she looked at him innocently. "What about it?"

"Let's start with why the hell you're wearing it after all these years."

Deliberately, she took a piece of cheese, biting into it. Knowing she was probably annoying him, she couldn't help it. While he was direct, stalling was her specialty. In fact, she had perfected it into an art form with her father. She swallowed again at Nico's serious face. Better not to press her luck with his interrogation.

"I've worn it off and on since you gave it to me, Nico. I can't explain. Things have been so out of control lately. To be honest, it brings me back to a time I felt safe and loved." She shrugged, for once not caring what he thought. It was the truth, and besides, it was her business!

He leaned back, his eyes widening. Picking up his glass, he took a big sip of his wine. Gazing off into the distance, he seemed to be deep in thought, his face impassive. Finally, he spoke, almost in wonderment. "I have never given a ring to another woman."

Georgie stared at his face, the lump in her throat too large to respond. He looked almost vulnerable. Relief washed over her as she realized how little she knew about his dating life. Turning his gaze back to her, his eyes hardened.

"But you have accepted another man's ring. That's why I am surprised you still have that cheap promise ring hanging around your neck. It was a long time ago."

Her hand immediately went to her throat. Too late, she realized she had deliberately not put it back on. "It wasn't cheap!"

"Georgie, I saw the giant diamond the Duke or Lord or whatever he was gave you! If you tried to wear that on a chain, you would topple over!"

Biting back a giggle at his exaggerated statement, it was now her turn to be surprised. "What are you on about? How do you know what my ring looked like?"

Nico regarded her steadily. Taking another sip of wine, he now seemed to be the one stalling. Finally, he looked at her directly. "Because I was there when he proposed."

Georgie stared at him incredulously. "Wait, what? You were there in the restaurant!" She paused for a moment, thinking back. "I knew it! You *were* there."

"How did you know? You didn't see me. You only had eyes for Bernard," he scoffed.

"Benjamin," she corrected automatically.

Taking a deep breath, she knew it was time to clear the air once and for all. "We were at the restaurant with friends. Well, you know that if you were there. I didn't know Benjamin was going to propose. It came out of nowhere. And afterwards, my friend Mary told me that she thought she saw you. Of course, she had only seen photos of you, but she described you perfectly." Georgie didn't add that Mary had said it was the hottest guy she had ever seen. And that he had stood frozen, his Mediterranean skin looking almost ashen, watching the spectacle.

Georgie leaned forward. "I ran outside. I even asked the porter, but no one saw which way you went. I can't explain it, but I felt your presence, Nico. I knew it had to be you."

He grimaced. "Earlier that evening, I went to your home and met your father. He wasn't very...welcoming, you could say. He told me where you were if I really wanted to see you. He also told me about Sir Benny and that you were serious. I was hoping he was wrong. That perhaps if we saw each other...I was so naïve."

"You weren't naïve," Georgie whispered.

"Georgie, the guy was on one knee, holding up the biggest rock I had ever seen. You didn't even look like yourself. You were in this mini sparkly dress. Your hair was even different—it was straight! You had on so much makeup I barely recognized you. Your friends were all the same. They were all in their fancy clothes. I felt like some *contadino*."

"Nico, you have never been a farmer! And why are you deliberately overlooking that you happen to be a member of one of the wealthiest families in Italy?"

He shook his head. "It's different. We weren't raised with wealth. And we have no titles. Your father looked at me like I was a cockroach he wanted to scrape off his shoe."

Georgie felt tears well up in her eyes. "I'm so sorry, Nico. If I could change things, I would. But my father didn't control my heart. He just tried to control the situation. Looking back, he must have known Benjamin was going to propose and you might witness it."

Nico ran a frustrated hand through his hair. His entire demeanor had changed and now he looked angry. Perhaps reliving it all brought back the terrible memories.

Georgie reached over and put her hand over his. The electricity was still there, like always. Could he feel it, too? "Nico, listen to me. I was going through a lot. I didn't know who I was or what I wanted. Throughout my entire life I was told what to do. The lines blurred between what I was told to do and what I *wanted* to do. I realized after a lot of soul searching, and a lot of flying, that the reason I loved my summers in Sicily was because I was just myself. I didn't have to be someone else."

He looked at her speculatively. "That was the only reason?"

"Of course not," she replied earnestly. "You were a big part of that time in my life. But I needed to know who I was. You had it all figured out. You knew what your passion was, what you loved doing. Look at all this." She stopped and waved around. "You described this perfectly to me a decade ago. I couldn't tell you anything about what I wanted. I shrunk into the person I thought everyone wanted me to be."

"So you accepted the ring from Duke Brandon?"

Georgie gave a frustrated sigh. "Will you just forget about all that duke nonsense? Who really cares? Yes, I accepted. It seemed the easiest way to go along with what everyone expected. A rich, handsome man wanted to marry me, so yes, I went along with it. Call me mad."

Nico slowly withdrew his hand, averting his gaze. His face registered sadness. Finally, he looked at her. "*Mi dispiace*, Georgie. It isn't my right at all to question you. You were free to marry whoever you wanted. We hadn't been together for years. We hadn't even talked for years. Of course, you should have accepted if you loved him."

Georgie relaxed a little at his softened tone. She wanted to tell him how much she hated the public display that night that made her even more pressured about saying yes. Instead, she stated the obvious: "Only I didn't love him. At least not in that way. It was a mistake, Nico."

When he remained silent, she continued. "After we got engaged, it all became a blur of plans and dress fittings—his mother, my mother, flowers, caterers. It wasn't my wedding; it just became *the* wedding. I was just swept up in the whole affair. I used to escape by taking a flying lesson just to think about anything other than the wedding."

"Why didn't you break it off?"

Georgie rubbed her forehead. "I was going to so many times. I thought I could go through with it. I thought I *should* go through with it."

Nico sat forward, gazing intently at her. "What happened on your wedding day, Georgie?"

She looked at him uneasily. "I felt your presence again. I can't quite explain it. I even found myself looking for you. That's when I realized you can't become someone's wife when you're thinking about another man. The night before the wedding, I almost called you. I sat there with my phone in hand, staring at it for ages before I finally persuaded myself not to do it. That's not a good sign, though, is it?"

At his silence, she continued. "So, when I entered the cathedral, it all came rushing at me. I asked to see Benjamin, and I told him I couldn't do it. The remarkable thing was he didn't even try to stop me." She gave a bitter laugh. "I don't know who was more relieved. That's when he told me he always knew he was competing with you. My father had let on about us. Funny enough, he told me to come find you. I guess he loved me enough to want me to be happy."

Nico smiled for the first time in hours. "Benji is growing on me. What happened then?"

Georgie winced. "The headlines were brutal. My father was humiliated. My mother was remarkably calm. I almost think she was relieved as well."

"Why didn't you call me if you were thinking about me?"

Georgie looked down at her lap. "As luck would have it, I saw a photo of you online from Marco's wedding. You had your arm around a woman, and you were both laughing. You appeared happy and in love. So, I couldn't chance it. There was no way I could take another humiliation. That's when I realized it was all just a one-sided fantasy. You probably hadn't been there the night I got engaged. It was all in my head, and I knew I had to move on. You obviously already had."

Nico's brows were drawn together and he looked lost in thought. "I didn't bring a date to Marco's wedding."

Georgie dug her phone out of her pocket. "I saved it. I wanted to remind myself when I was feeling weak that you were with someone." She scrolled through her photos and finally turned it toward him.

Nico burst out laughing. He laughed so hard he snorted. "I'm sorry, Georgie. That's a photo of my sister-in-law."

"Marco's wife?"

"No, the other one. Katie married Marco. Her best friend Teresa was her maid of honor. Teresa later married my brother Stefano."

Georgie stared at him in disbelief and then back at the photo. "But you look so...cozy."

Nico smirked. "I was making mischief. I knew Stefano was already interested in Teresa, though he wouldn't admit it. I was doing some harmless flirting just to get him riled up. My life's goal is to irritate my brothers. It took a little while, but it worked."

She slid the phone back in her pocket, and they stared at each other. He smiled gently at her. "So there's no Benjamin. And there's no woman on my side. There never was. I'm pretty good at math, Georgie. That just leaves you and me."

"What are you saying?"

He scraped his chair back, standing and coming over to her. He helped her stand, and he was so close she could smell his spicy cologne. Putting a gentle arm around her, he was careful not to touch her cast. Her heart was racing, and her mind was having a hard time keeping up with matters. Suddenly, feeling almost shy, she couldn't look at him but stared at his shirt buttons. He put a gentle hand under her chin, and she was forced to see his loving expression. How long had it been since he looked at her like that?

"I'm in love with you, George. I always have been."

Tears welled in her eyes. "Oh, Nico, I love you, too. I am so sorry."

"Sorry about what?"

"Everything. Our past, my stupid mistakes."

His mouth lowered inches from hers. "Be quiet, George."

His lips descended to take hers. This time, she didn't pull

back. She gave as much as he did. His hands moved to cup her face, and he kissed her like a man who was starving. Slowly, he stopped and stared before he swept in again and gave her a series of thorough kisses. She felt herself melting, and he seemed to sense it. "Let's go inside," he said huskily.

"Where to?" she whispered.

"To find that ring."

sixteen

Georgie grinned at Nico as he stood in the kitchen, wearing his usual faded jeans and T-shirt. He looked years younger this morning, his hair still a little disheveled. She couldn't keep her hands from running through it all night. Their desire had been insatiable, and they hadn't been able to keep their hands off each other. It had been the most tender and passionate night of her life, and she felt a sense of wholeness.

Finally their hunger got the best of them. They were in the kitchen, rummaging through the pantry for sustenance. Nico smiled at her, swooping in for a quick kiss. "There isn't much. Today is Angelina's shopping day."

"I thought you called her and told her not to come in."

He grinned, his dimples flashing. "I did. I want you all to myself, at least while we are home. I gave the entire staff the day off."

She gave him a mocking frown. "Are you planning on starving me?"

He laughed, hugging her tighter. "Well, if you insist on eating, we'll have to take a brief journey into town. I guess I can share you awhile. I want to show you Taormina anyway. You've never been there, have you?"

Georgie shook her head, reaching up to kiss his deep dimple. Her lips moved across it and then his jaw. She worked her way toward his mouth and she felt his breath quicken.

"George," he muttered. "This will not get you food anytime soon."

"Don't care," she whispered.

He lifted her onto the farmhouse kitchen table so he could get a better angle on her mouth. Finally, he withdrew a little, but she clutched onto the front of his shirt. He gave her a heated stare. "Do you want to go to Taormina?"

"Later," she breathed, drawing his head down.

"THIS LOOKS AMAZING!" Georgie exclaimed, staring at the wide glass of coffee *granita* the server set before her on the Italian ceramic table.

"There's more whipped cream on it than coffee," Nico noted, and then grinned at her cheerful expression. He sipped his small espresso, contently watching her enjoy the *granita*, taking delicate bites with a spoon. She watched him take yet another *brioscia*, from their basket and bite into it. They had both been starving, in more ways than one.

They were sitting at an outdoor café in Taormina after finally pulling themselves out of the house. Nico parked outside of the town, and they walked through the Porta Messina, a stone archway at the northern end of the city. Nico explained it was one of two gates built by the Arabs to protect the city. The town, perched high on the hilltop, offered sweeping views of the Ionian Sea and coastline. They had strolled through the narrow cobblestone streets and the quaint but beautiful *piazzas*. Nico promised they would visit some of the ancient ruins another day where they could see Mount Etna if the clouds cooperated. In a way it seemed to be a glamorous city, but still kept its quaintness. Georgie told him she couldn't wait to explore some of the medieval streets that looked charming as they walked by.

"I already adore it here," Georgie remarked, glancing around at all the climbing bougainvillea in the shops and the flowers bursting out of Italian pottery. "I can see why you do with all the flowers and plants!"

Nico smiled in response. Almost to reassure her, he covered her hand for a minute, stroking the palm. The small contact was all it took to ignite a wave of desire that traveled up her spine. Frowning, she said, "Nico, I can't eat this *granita* if you are holding my usable hand."

He threw his head back and laughed, releasing her. "Alright, *cara*, I promise not to touch you until the *granita* is finished."

Georgie grinned, taking another bite of the whipped cream and coffee ice. "This is heaven."

"You said that earlier when I was kissing your…"

"Nico! Shhh!" Georgie said, glancing frantically around.

"You're in Italy, George. No one would care if I grabbed you and kissed you for hours right here at this table."

She looked guiltily down at her *granita*. "Nico, I need to tell you something."

He took off his sunglasses, his eyes now wary. "I thought we talked through everything already."

It was true. They had talked for hours the night before when they could physically tear themselves away from each other. A lot of ground had been covered, and they both had admitted they carried too much of the past with them.

She smiled. "It's only a small thing. Remember when you kissed me at the *festa*?"

"George, it was a week ago. I remember. And I remember the look on your face. Frankly, I never want to see that expression again."

"What expression?"

He stared at her. "I couldn't tell if it was panic, revulsion or dismay. Because of that, I instantly regretted it."

"And then I broke my arm."

"And then you broke your arm. *Dio*, when you fell, I thought you hit your head. Everything from our past came rushing forward. At that moment, I knew at some point I had to tell you I loved you."

Georgie smiled sweetly at him, and he frowned. "Don't smile like that, George, or we are going to have to go home." He leaned back. "You were saying. What about that kiss?"

"I just wanted you to know that I *did* panic. You were right. I just thought that if everyone in town saw you kissing me, especially my mother, it would send the wrong message."

"Such as?" he asked with a mocking grin.

"Now you're teasing me," Georgie said. "I just wanted you to know that I wasn't rejecting you. I was planning on finding a way at some point to try to explain the past and ask for your forgiveness, at the very least."

"That's all you wanted was forgiveness?"

"Of course not."

He looked at her, smiling tenderly. "What do you want from me now?"

"Only your love."

"You've had that since the moment I laid eyes on you."

Georgie instantly felt like the luckiest woman in the world. "Let's go home." Glancing down at the *granita*, she sighed. "Right after I finish this!"

GEORGIE LET Nico lead her down yet another alley. They had torn themselves away from each other to return to Taormina for dinner. Nico insisted he wanted to take her out on a real date. Dressed in a light blue halter dress which Nico had taken great pleasure in tying, she felt somewhat put together. The only downside was her hair. Angelina wasn't there to help her fix it, yet Nico told her he loved it no matter what. Frowning in the mirror, she had insisted at least she wear it in a ponytail to get it out of her way. Laughter had bubbled up as she watched Nico concentrating on gathering all her hair in one ponytail tie. It had taken several attempts before he was satisfied. Georgie couldn't resist teasing him. "This could be your backup career!"

His response was to give her ponytail a little yank like he was a schoolboy. She smiled. How many little girls had he taunted as a young boy?

Traveling through the cobblestone streets of Taormina, they strolled this time through the impressive stone archway of the Porta Catania. Wandering through a few shops, Georgie admired all the Italian pottery and linens. The shopkeepers greeted Nico by first name, and he proudly introduced her to so many people her head was spinning. It was obvious he was well known and beloved throughout the town.

"Ah, here we are. This is a wonderful restaurant," Nico said, stopping to usher her inside its cool interior.

An older man rushed over. "Niccolo, we didn't know you were in town," he said, staring obviously at Georgie.

"Just for a few days, Antonio," Nico answered, turning to introduce Georgie. She accepted the man's kiss on each cheek and followed him to a corner table, which overlooked the sea. As she glanced down at the printed menu sheet, she couldn't help but notice the exorbitant prices and the extravagant gourmet offerings. She tended to avoid places like this. Looking up, she encountered Nico's stare. "What?" Putting a hand on her hair, she said, "My hair looks ridiculous, doesn't it? I should have worn it down."

He laughed. "Absolutely not. *Bella.* You look beautiful,

George. I was just thinking about how many times I thought of us like this. Grownups on a proper date."

"You took me to restaurants when we were younger."

He shook his head. "We were babies, and they were all casual restaurants. I wanted to take you somewhere like this."

The elegant tables were adorned with crisp white linens, shining silver, and stunning floral arrangements. Their fellow diners were just as impressive, dressed in designer and formal wear. Even Nico tonight wore a black jacket and pressed slacks with a crisp button-down shirt.

"Nico, this is lovely, but honestly, I don't mind where we go."

"It matters to me," he said firmly.

The server appeared, and he ordered a bottle of prosecco, before turning his attention back to her. "Tonight, we are celebrating."

She smiled. "What are we celebrating? That we managed to leave the house?"

He returned her grin. "It was touch and go! But yes, we are celebrating our new beginning."

She twisted the stem of her water glass, her gaze averted. He reached over and stilled her hand. "What are you nervous about?"

"That we can't forget the past," she said frankly.

The server appeared then, and they both waited silently for him to open the bottle, pour two glasses, and nestle it into the wine cooler before departing.

Nico's gaze never left hers, and the heat rose. All he had to do was look at her like that. He picked up his glass. "We can, and we will," he declared. "Here's to our new start, George."

"To a new start," she echoed, clinking her glass with his. She took a sip and forced a smile. A subtle gnawing sensation was stirring within her, only to fade away moments later as she soaked in his happiness.

seventeen

Georgie sat on the bench, her chin in her hand, waiting. Nico had gone in search of refreshing drinks. They had spent the morning investigating all the nooks and crannies of Taormina, and Georgie enjoyed walking through all the alleys and shops. They had come upon an exclusive four-star hotel that had been used as a backdrop in a television series. Nico suggested they return to lunch there, but Georgie gently dismissed the idea. It concerned her that Nico assumed that was the kind of place she needed to be taken to. It was difficult to shake off the feeling of unease. Should she tell him she would rather eat a *panino* on a bench? It didn't matter, just as long as he was there.

With her arm aching a little, Georgie asked if they could sit for a while in the *Piazza IX Aprile*, with its checkerboard walkway. Sitting on the bench, she marveled at the *Torre dell'Orologio*, a majestic stone clock tower. Two Italian musicians played accordions merrily to the crowd, and Georgie soaked in the joyful atmosphere. Ships glided in the blue sea below them, and Georgie swept her hair back as the wind teased it.

A familiar shadow blocked out the sun. *"Grazie,"* Georgie

said with a smile, accepting the cup of fresh pomegranate juice Nico handed her. Taking a long sip, she watched a group of young children stroll by in a ragged line, loosely following the directions of the accompanying teachers. The girls held hands, giggling and talking, while the boys shoved and teased each other.

"That's you right there," Georgie said, pointing to one of the small boys wearing a cap, who remarkably looked like Nico. "I can imagine you at that age. Probably yanking some poor girl's ponytail."

Nico grinned. "I was always into mischief. My mother will delight in telling you some of my finest moments," he said dryly.

"I already heard some of them," Georgie answered without thinking.

He turned and stared at her, a light in his eyes. "This time will be different, though. I will be with you. I've longed to take you home to meet my family. Can we do it after your check-up in Palermo?"

She smiled contently, leaning her head on his shoulder. "Of course. I'd love to."

"You can even meet Teresa, who you were so jealous of."

She nudged him with her uninjured elbow. "Not funny. Don't mess about."

He grinned tenderly down at her. "It just makes me a little happy that you were jealous. Even if there was no reason to be."

She looked up at him anxiously. She saw something in his eyes—the old hurt glinted and vanished. Perhaps they were being foolish. They couldn't erase the past.

"Nico," she said hesitantly.

He stood abruptly. "The surprise is here!"

Georgie looked around, confused. A small Fiat, painted wildly in a variety of bright colors, drove toward them. After parking, a young man got out, a huge smile on his face.

Georgie stood and walked slowly around the little car. A picnic basket was strapped to its back.

"We're taking the Taormina car out for a spin and a picnic. It's getting crowded here," he explained while guiding her into her seat. Leaning in to give her a quick kiss, he assisted her with her seatbelt before running around to the driver's side.

George laughed as he squeezed into the little car. There was hardly room for them both. Nico slowly began to drive away, and the crowds automatically parted for the little car as they navigated the narrow streets. They were forced to stop frequently for people to take photos. Apparently, it was famous around town and was often captured on social media by tourists. Soon, however, they were out the Porta Messina and climbed the hill.

"I know just the spot," Nico told her, as they came upon a garden overlooking the sea. When he parked, Georgie didn't wait for Nico to come around to her side. She got out gingerly, looking around. Taormina lay before them, the sea beyond.

"Oh, it's gorgeous up here!"

Nico spread a blanket under an olive tree and put the basket on it. He returned to the car and came back with a bottle of lemon seltzer and glasses.

Georgie laughed. "Where were those? There's hardly any room in that tiny car!"

They sat down and nibbled on all the small plates from the picnic basket, from melon wrapped with prosciutto, to fresh vegetables and cheese. The *Sfincione*, a focaccia-like pizza topped with fresh ripe tomatoes, was so light and pillowy that Georgie moaned. "Why does the bread taste so good here?"

Sipping their wine, Nico asked more about Georgie's job. It was wonderful to talk about it with him, as she finally felt the support she craved over the years about her becoming a pilot. She told him it was exciting for her to be a part of someone's medical journey. To know that because of her skills, a needed organ or a medical team was getting to a person who was in need.

As if he was reading her thoughts, Nico nuzzled her neck. "I'm really proud of you, George. I often hoped you would find something that brought you joy. You're so smart."

Georgie turned to look at him incredulously.

He stared at her, confused. "Why are you looking at me like that?"

She turned her gaze away, suddenly embarrassed. "No one has ever told me that."

"But you must know that! You always excelled at school."

Georgie shrugged. "School isn't life. Until I realized that flying was my passion, I felt like I was failing at life."

He smiled and put an arm around her. "I've felt that way at times as well." He dropped a kiss on her head. "But guess what? I think we are on a clear path upward."

Georgie smiled and gently sunk down on the blanket with her arm around his neck. Everything suddenly seemed perfect.

THE NEXT FEW days went by quickly. Nico seemed to have a never-ending supply of surprises up his sleeve, always striving to make her time as perfect as possible. Georgie was divided on enjoying them but also trying to best determine how to tell him they weren't necessary. She was just as happy staying at home, snuggling with him on the outdoor chaise, overlooking the blue sea. Watching him dig and discuss his thoughts enthusiastically with the gardener was her morning routine she looked forward to. Fun for her was seeing him swim, gliding through the water effortlessly before he inevitably stopped to heave himself up and kiss her as she sat on the side. Those times together were the ones she would cherish.

One surprise she enjoyed immensely was their trip to the

opera at the Teatro Greco. Visiting the ancient Greek theater at sunset in Taormina was extraordinary. Bathed in the warm glow of the setting sun, they marveled at the majestic outline of Mount Etna in the distance, as they soaked in the music under the stars.

The more formal events were less enjoyable. Since the town was known for being a retreat for celebrities, artists and writers, there were exclusive resorts and restaurants in abundance. They dined at some of Taormina's select restaurants where people spoke in hush tones, and Georgie felt like she had to sit up straight. Presented with *Spaghetti ai Ricci di Mare*, which was exquisitely prepared, she longed for the dishes she craved. It was more difficult not to think of the poor sea urchin as she ate it. She tried not to gaze longingly as they walked past the more casual *osterias* where people dined outside, obviously having a wonderful time, shouting with laughter. She was envious watching them eat *Pasta 'Ncasciata*, a Sicilian baked rigatoni dish bursting with flavor from tomatoes, aubergine and buttery caciocavallo cheese or *Chicken Scarpariello*, with its bell peppers and tangy lemon sauce. Then there were the casual *pasticcerias* that featured *cannoli*, dripping with cheese and pistachios dotting the ends.

After they declared their love for each other, Georgie made a silent vow to follow Nico's lead, anxious about causing any dissention in their fresh bond. Her goal was to not let anything come between them, yet she shrunk into herself a little. Rationalizing that it was just for a while until he appeared more confident eased her wariness.

"You're not listening to a word I'm saying," Nico said accusingly.

Georgie startled and glanced over at him and then smiled sweetly. He looked so handsome sitting across from her in the villa's sunroom, his laptop open. They had enjoyed a leisurely morning, and Nico begged her forgiveness, declaring he needed to do some work. It had felt good to have a little time to herself, and Georgie made some calls while upstairs, starting with her job. Her boss was still understanding, agreeing that obviously she needed to heal before resuming her flight schedule. The next call was to her mother, who complained she had heard so little from her. Georgie apologized and finally admitted she and Nico had reconciled.

Now, with Nico staring at her, she felt herself blush. "I'm sorry. I was just thinking. I called my mother earlier, and she didn't seem too surprised that you and I are back together. I never asked how you two became so friendly."

His expression turned a little guilty. "Your mother wasn't as fierce as I thought she was going to be. If you want the truth, I used two parts charm, one part honesty. I think she realized how deep my feelings were for you, even if I didn't come right out and tell her."

"She seems to really like you."

"My family's money probably doesn't hurt," Nico said dryly.

Georgie rushed to her mother's defense. "Nico, she's not like that! Honestly, my mother is more of a literary snob. And while she might have wanted to leave her roots behind, she's not impressed by wealth just for the sake of it. I've seen her brush off some very important people simply because she didn't like them."

"Then how does she live with your father?" Nico asked shortly.

Georgie sighed and sunk deeper into the couch. "Well, that's probably why he's living in Paris on his own, and she's chosen to stay in England."

Nico sat straighter, putting the laptop aside. "*Mi Dispiace*, George. I did not know. What is your father doing in Paris?"

Georgie fidgeted with a string on her shorts. "He's the ambassador to France," she finally admitted.

"*Scusa?*"

"You heard me. He's settled into his residence in Paris and seems to be doing well." Georgie shrugged. "I really don't want to talk about my father. We're not very close."

Standing up, she glanced toward the kitchen. "So, what's for lunch?"

Nico stared at her for a minute, as if choosing whether to continue the conversation. "Angelina came by with some groceries. I asked her to pick up some fried eggplant."

"We call it aubergine at home," Georgie said with a smile. "That sounds lovely!"

He smiled. "I saw the way you were eying it at the outdoor cafes we passed. That, along with some of the other dishes."

"I admit it did catch my eye! I thought it looked delicious. I never ate it until *Nonna* cooked it for me. I haven't had it in ages," Georgie explained.

Nico studied her intently, as if he was assessing something. Feeling uncertain, she walked over and nestled in his lap, her one arm sliding around his neck. His lips immediately met hers in a searing kiss. The man could kiss. That was simply a fact. After a few minutes, he finally raised his head, breathing hard. "Are you trying to distract me?"

She pulled his head down and gave him a soft kiss. "Just for a few minutes. Then I'm going to tuck into all that fried eggplant."

His answer was to descend upon her lips until she forgot all about lunch.

eighteen

It was evening and Georgie was enjoying sitting outside enjoying the view with Nico until his phone buzzed. "*Mi dispiace,* I have to take this." Raising his phone, he said, "*Pronto.*"

He stood and walked away. Georgie knew enough Italian to follow along. However, Nico seemed to be doing more listening than talking. When he spoke, he wandered away farther into the garden, almost as if he didn't want her to hear the conversation. It was ridiculous to be paranoid. Nico wouldn't hide anything from her, right?

He walked toward her, putting his phone in his shorts pocket. Sitting, he smiled at her. "Let's talk about what I was going to bring up earlier," he said, apparently not intending to discuss the phone call. "Your follow-up appointment in Palermo is in three days."

Georgie raised her cast a little. "The doctor said they would probably be able to put a shorter cast on. It will be nice if it's lighter."

"I know you can't wait to be finished with the entire ordeal," Nico agreed. "But since we'll be in Palermo, I was thinking that perhaps we should stay in the city for a night or so. And then we probably should return to Nizza to make some decisions on *Nonno*'s land before going to my mother's."

"What kind of decisions?"

"I'm going to spend a day evaluating the crops with another of Oro Industries' agronomists. I trust Giovanni's opinions."

Georgie tried not to feel a little hurt. "Am I included?" As he narrowed his eyes at her tone, she continued, choosing her words more carefully. "What I mean to say is that as a co-owner, I'd like to hear what you have to say about the state of the crops."

Nico nodded absentmindedly. "Of course."

"Returning to my original question. What decisions?"

"Oh, a whole list. State of the crops, sustainability options and irrigation. Boring stuff for you, I'm sure."

Did he sound condescending? It was probably her imagination. Before she could comment, he continued. "I have an idea. What if we depart tomorrow and take our time getting to Palermo?"

Georgie raised her eyebrows. "Take our time? It's only a few hours' drive."

He grinned with his dimples out in full force. "Not if you go by boat."

SITTING in a cushy lounge chair on the top deck of the mega yacht, Georgie relaxing under an umbrella. Nico stood in the distance, chatting and laughing with the Chief Steward. He finally turned and came back to sit near her. "Comfortable? You're not too hot out here?"

"No, it's lovely in the shade," Georgie said, glancing at him briefly. He looked so carefree in his khaki shorts and white shirt, his hair blowing in the wind. "And I'd much rather be out where I can take in the view. This isn't just a boat, Nico—it's the biggest yacht I've ever seen!"

He shrugged. "You've probably been on many. It's not mine; Marco owns it. I have a couple of jet boats just for my own use at the villa, but I don't know if I'd use a yacht that much. Marco generously shares it with the family."

Georgie looked at him warily. "Nico, I don't care if you have a yacht or a toy boat. You know that, don't you? I mean, this is wonderful, but it's unnecessary, if you see what I mean."

He took a sip of his craft beer, his eyes hidden by his sunglasses. "But you're having fun, right?"

"Of course I am! Who wouldn't? It's gorgeous!" Georgie reassured him. How could she make him understand that there was no need for all these extravagant gestures without sounding ungrateful?

Nico seemed to sense her wariness, for he began pointing out some attractions, telling her entertaining tales about their history. She had never seen Sicily from the water. It would be fantastic to sail around the entire island. Opening her mouth, she was about to tell him so, but he would take that as a hint, and the next thing she knew, he would book such a tour. She needed to tread lightly.

They dined on the deck that night, eating their way through an exquisite meal served by Marco's chef. She smiled when she saw the *Pasta 'Ncasciata, Chicken Scarpariello,* and pistachio *cannoli,* realizing she must have an expressive face. And she was enchanted when tiny fairy lights turned on as dusk settled in. As the music filled the air from hidden speakers, Nico pulled her close to dance. She put her uninjured arm around his neck and wished they could nuzzle closer without a sling in the way. Reading her mind, his hot breath was close to her ear. "Just a couple more days, George."

Nodding, she leaned into him. If only time could slow down. Everything seemed so perfect. Too perfect. Why did it seem like a clock was ticking down to the moment when she would lose it all?

nineteen

"It feels so much better," Georgie said, gingerly lifting her arm as she sat on the exam room's table. The cast was much smaller, ending at her elbow. She didn't need the sling, and the doctor had been satisfied with her results. When they had changed casts and taken x-rays, her arm had looked so pale and withered. She would have to slowly build it back up once the final cast was removed. The doctor promised it would be only another month or so before leaving to go find a nurse to bring in the paperwork.

Nico was leaning against the wall watching her closely after questioning the doctor extensively about her recovery. On the yacht, he mentioned that he wanted to fly in the specialist again to take another look, but Doctor Maloberti was on another case in Spain. Georgie assured him that the orthopedic doctor in Palermo would be just fine.

Though she was eager for the appointment, leaving the luxurious yacht was difficult. It had been a wonderful three days of just sailing slowly toward Palermo. Nico seemed more like himself, riding the jet ski completely carefree, taunting her with daredevil moves until she laughingly covered her eyes and shrieked. They explored the ship, and she was allowed to go up to the helm and meet the captain. They watched movies in the ship's theater and relaxed for hours in the shade. Most of all, they had long conversations. Of course, they had many years to catch up on, but now they shared deeper thoughts. Georgie felt she could finally be honest about her father and their relationship. Nico was sympathetic to a point. She could still tell the old hurt was there, that her father had purposely sent him to witness her engagement.

Nico worked a couple hours each day, and Georgie also finally logged into her own business account and began attacking her email. She was beyond grateful to the other pilots who had stepped in and taken her workload. But it gave her pause. How were she and Nico going to handle it when she returned to London? They hadn't talked about that or really what their future was. Georgie had been at the point of bringing it up several times, only to bite her tongue. The priority was for them to stay grounded in the present.

"What are you thinking about over there?" Nico asked, pushing against the wall and coming toward her. "You're not in pain?"

"Goodness, no," Georgie said, smiling at him. "Honestly, it feels so much more comfortable. I just want to get out of here."

On cue, the nurse walked in with an envelope, handing it to Georgie and reminding her that the doctor would be happy to consult with whoever she saw for her last appointment when she returned to London. Georgie avoided looking at Nico at the mention of her going home.

Offering her his hand so she could hop down from the examining table, she automatically raised her face for his swift kiss. She heard the nurse sigh, and she almost smiled. Sometimes she couldn't believe how fortunate she was either.

They walked out of the hospital, and Nico smiled at her as

they got into his rich blue Alfa Romeo. She had been surprised when he mentioned his car was waiting for them when they came ashore. Logistical things seemed to effortlessly fall into place for him, as if by magic.

They drove into the heart of the city, and Nico pulled up to an exclusive hotel, where the valet was waiting to greet them. The intricately designed building was once a palace before becoming a five-star hotel. As Nico helped her out of the car, she smiled up at him. "Remember the hotel we spent the night in when the storm hit?"

He grimaced. "How could I forget? I thought we were going to get bedbugs."

She frowned. "Nico, it was the most romantic hotel in the world."

He shook his head, not looking at her. "Hardly. I couldn't believe that's where I had to take you. All the hotels were already full. I was embarrassed."

She put her hand in his, making him stop walking. "Well, I wasn't. I just wanted to be with you. And if I recall, you weren't...quite as romantic as I'd hoped you would be."

He smiled gently, putting a strand of hair behind her ear, and giving her a soft kiss. "We've talked about that, George. You know I was trying to be a gentleman, as well as stay alive. *Nonno* would have murdered me. But to answer your original question, I remember every second of that night."

She smiled sweetly at him, and he bent to kiss her, harder this time.

"Let's go make some more memories," he said huskily.

"ARE WE LATE FOR DINNER?" Georgie asked anxiously, as Nico pulled her through the crowds and down the street. He glanced back to smile but kept walking at a fast pace.

Georgie noticed Nico repeatedly glanced at his silver watch in their hotel suite after he dressed in black pants and a crisp gray shirt. He looked elegant and handsome. She wore what he had deemed his favorite, a deep blue sundress, with simple cap sleeves and a V-neck that showed a little cleavage. The sun had kissed her face and arms, so she only used minimal makeup. For once, her hair was behaving. Nico had only gazed at her heatedly before pulling her out of the suite, muttering about being late. At the pace they were now walking, she was happy she wore low-heeled wedge sandals. Suddenly, he stopped so abruptly she almost ran into his back.

"Nico, what on earth?" she protested. He turned to her, blocking her view. Peeping around him, she saw the marquee that read: *Opera dei Pupi.*

"Oh, Nico, the puppet show! Are we going?" she asked excitedly. She had shared with him her mother's special memory of seeing it with her parents.

His answer was to grin, grabbing her hand and leading her in. She stood in the cramped lobby as he bought tickets, and they quickly found seats in the small theater. Glancing around, she saw rows of puppets or *pupi* hanging on the wall. Their costumes were detailed and meticulously crafted, showcasing armored soldiers, priests, and maidens.

"How did you know I wanted to come here so badly?" Georgie asked, turning to look at his pleased expression.

"I should have thought of it before hearing your story," he confessed. "It's such a large part of Sicilian culture. I remember my mother talking about how she and my father went to one on their honeymoon. I've actually always wanted to go, too!"

Georgie grinned, happy that Nico was as excited about it as she was. The audience was mainly adults, and a hush came upon them as the lights dimmed. For the next forty-five minutes, Georgie watched transfixed as the story unfolded. Knights fearlessly battled for the maiden's honor in a rather violent love story interjected with humor. The sound of the narration in Italian filled the air, blending with the powerful music that rose to a dramatic climax as the knights unsheathed their swords, battling furiously. Georgie understood most of the storytelling, the Sicilian dialect coming back to her now that she was immersed in it. Every time she glanced happily at Nico, his gaze was on her. She grabbed his hand to let him know how much she appreciated going to the show.

When the lights came on and the puppeteers appeared and bowed to a standing ovation, Georgie remarked to Nico that they looked like giants on the small stage. For a time, she had almost forgotten that humans were working the complicated strings and rods to make the *pupi* spring to life.

"That was amazing!" Georgie exclaimed, turning to Nico. He threw his arm around her, kissing the top of her head. "Do you want to go see them up close?"

"Can I?" Her eyes widened. He smiled gently, leading her toward the stage. They waited their turn, and she was allowed to gently lift one of the *pupi*, which was a knight. It was heavier than she thought, and Nico took photos of her as she laughed at the weight. She gently handed the knight back to the puppeteer, who was already preparing to do another show.

As they left the theater, Georgie was elated. The two of them shared this memory, but she could also now discuss it with her mother. Linking her arm through Nico's, she smiled up at him, but he was glancing at his watch again. The show was over. What else required timing? It must not have been anything because his gait remained slow. They strolled through the crowded street, stopping every so often to look at street vendors selling Italian pottery and trinkets. Georgie glanced over at a *salumi* with outdoor tables and abundant *antipasto* boards. Her mouth watered looking at the eggplant. Nico followed her glance and put an arm around her. "Don't worry. We'll have eggplant at dinner!"

He stopped to browse through more Italian tourist items, which puzzled her. "Are you looking for a gift or something?"

"No, just looking around," he said absentmindedly. He looked at his phone, and then he grabbed her hand. "Let's go to dinner."

They walked toward *I Quattro Canti*, and it was just as she remembered it when she was a teenager. Twirling slowly, she looked at the Baroque architecture and the facades on the four buildings. It took a minute, but then her gaze finally focused on the last corner, where tall, colorful Italian vases had been placed to block off an area. A red rope was at the entrance, and a man in a black suit smiled at them. As they approached, he disengaged the rope. Georgie looked down at the rose petals at her feet, ruby red against the gray cobblestone. Now at dusk, the area was illuminated by the soft glow of candles flickering among the dozens of long-stem red roses in vases everywhere. Music began, and a woman on a keyboard sang, "What a wonderful world." People stopped walking to stare.

Blood rushed to her head, and she was dizzy and queasy all at once. "Nico," she whispered. He was down on one knee, a ring box open in his hand.

"George," he said, looking at her tenderly. "We have come full circle, back to the spot where I first told you I loved you. I was a boy, and now I am a man. I couldn't love you anymore than I do now. We have been through so much together, but we have come out the other side, stronger and more resilient. You are everything to me, Georgie. Will you become my wife?"

People watched around them. An uncomfortable déjà vu almost came upon her. She quickly dismissed it because this proposal, while still public, was from Nico.

"Of course," she whispered, grinning. He stood and swept her up, hugging her tightly. The crowd burst into applause and shouted words of good fortune in Italian.

Georgie smiled from Nico's arms and then went back to

kissing him. They stopped to both glance down at her hand, admiring the enormous square diamond, with additional pave diamonds on the band. It was perfect, she told herself. There was no reason to feel any doubt about their relationship. So why did it keep creeping into her thoughts?

twenty

Georgie smiled as she admired her new ring. While it was bigger and grander than what she would have selected, she knew Nico was proud of it. He had protested that she still wore the promise ring on her right hand, but she told him she couldn't bear to part with it.

Glancing out the window of Nico's car, she watched the fields of green grass that swept downward toward the crystal blue sea. They were headed to Nizza to make decisions about the farm before going to Nico's family's estate.

It was difficult to leave Palermo. They spent a leisurely morning admiring the Teatro Massimo, one of the largest opera houses in Europe. Nico promised to take Georgie there sometime, remembering how fondly his mother spoke of going to the opera there on her honeymoon. They meandered through the historic and vibrant streets, laughing at how intricate ancient buildings stood proudly next to balconies with hanging laundry. Georgie loved the vibrant energy and was excited when they came upon a large chaotic street market. Nico immediately was drawn in, becoming animated as he surveyed the fresh produce. He spoke with some of the vendors about their agricultural conditions. At first, Georgie had been patient, but when her nose twitched at a familiar scent, she dragged Nico away to find a wide array of street food. He had explained earlier that morning that the island's food scene reflected the architecture—the many prior civilizations that once called Sicily home. When she had asked him how he knew so much about it, he told her laughingly she would understand once he met his foodie brother, Stefano.

As they walked through the market, music blared from speakers as the workers danced behind their kiosks or shouted for them to stop and buy their delectable food. The smell of spices and seafood filled the air and Georgie surveyed the *arancini*, fried rice balls, sometimes stuffed with meat that Nico told her was invented to be a portable dish for hungry workers. They ate those, along with fresh tomatoes and *burrata*, and fried artichokes. Then Nico insisted on a cannoli taste test, with them debating which was the best. It had all been delicious.

As he drove, they were both quiet now, relishing in the scenery. Glancing at her, he gave her a quick smile. "Did you enjoy Palermo?"

"How could I not? It was perfect, Nico. We had such a brilliant time. I can't wait to go back again."

The winding road held Nico's attention, but she saw a dimple appear. "There's a lot more to see. And a lot more of Sicily as well. I want to show it all to you, George."

Georgie frowned a little. There was that feeling again. "Nico, we probably need to talk about the future. I mean, where will we live? And what about my job? I could look for something similar here."

Nico shrugged. "There's time for us to talk about that. We have time. And of course I'm supportive of your choice to be a pilot, but I have to admit it's hard to get used to the idea."

Georgie frowned a little, but he continued quickly. "And we will have to decide if we want to split our time between my houses or just settle in one."

"How many do you have?"

"Just five," he said, handling a turn with ease.

"Five?" Georgie shouted. "Nico, why do you have so many?"

He shrugged. "Investments, in part. I travel a lot, Georgie. Though now I will turn over more of my duties at Oro Industries to privately consult. I want to help local farmers, especially here in Sicily. They have done things the same for centuries and it will take convincing, but they need to evolve and relearn everything."

She smiled at him. "I think that's lovely, Nico. Some of those farmers today sounded like they are really struggling, especially with increased heat."

He nodded. "They have to learn new ways to manage and what regenerative farming can do for their crops. It will take some convincing. But I don't need the money. I'd like to just travel around and help them."

"So we would live in Taormina?"

"Well, not necessarily. We could live there part-time I guess, and then if we want, we can even build a villa on my family's estate. I'll show you the property that my mother gifted me. We all have several hectares."

The powerful car was climbing the hill in Nizza easily as they approached her grandparents' home. Georgie felt the grief come back in a sharp wave. It must have hit Nico as well, for he cleared his throat a couple of times. Finally, he spoke. "Have you thought about what you want to do with the house?"

Georgie looked out the window at the rows of lemon trees they were passing. She felt the lump in her throat grow just thinking about it. "I don't know. It's not really practical to live there, but the thought of it just sitting empty breaks my heart as well." Georgie sniffed before continuing. "There are so many memories. If I were to sell it, I would need to at least move a few things out of it. Of course, the boxes of photos and things like *Nonno's* rocking chair. But it means so much to me. I don't think I can let it go, Nico."

His hand slid over hers. "Then you don't have to, George. How about we keep it as our little getaway?"

She gave him a smile. He always knew the exact thing to say to make her feel better. "That would be lovely," she said, her voice husky. "Have I told you how much I love you?"

He parked the car and turned toward her, taking his sunglasses off. He grinned at her. "Yes, but you can start from the beginning again."

~

THE NEXT DAY, Georgie forgot about her previous declaration that Nico always knew what to say to make her feel better. To say she was now annoyed with him was putting it lightly.

The day started early with meeting Giovanni at the original lemon grove. From there, they had toured the entire property. Giovanni wasn't much older than Nico and was very kind, apologizing quickly that he was not fluent in English. Therefore, the two men primarily spoke in Italian most of the day. While Georgie's comprehension had returned, they spoke in such technical terms that she easily became lost. Using her translator app on her phone, she was able to absorb some of it. But by the time she looked up words such as pathogens, carbon and nitrogen, they had moved on. Nico was so focused on the conversation most of the day, he spent little time explaining things to her. Georgie understood it would be difficult to completely teach her everything in one day, but she still was peeved that Nico didn't even try.

In fact, at one point she stopped to question them about fertilizer. Nico patiently explained that, of course, they used only organic fertilization on the crops. "I know that, Nico," Georgie said, trying to keep the edge out of her voice, but failing. "What I'm asking is, what exactly are you using?"

He then went on to tell her, but she had already sensed the patronizing undertone. It was almost as if he was trying to infer that she keep her nose out of her own crops.

Walking into the house after the long day, Georgie kicked off her dusty work boots. Nico was still outside, laughing away with Giovanni. She went to the sink to get a glass of cold water. It would help her cool off, and she needed to in more ways than one.

"Hey, George, get me a glass, will you?" Nico requested as he entered the kitchen from behind her. Automatically, she grabbed a glass from the nearby cabinet and filled it. "Do you want some ice?"

"Of course," he said.

"Of course? What do you mean, of course? How would I know you want ice?" Georgie sounded completely unreasonable, but she couldn't help it. Putting ice in the glass, she thrust it at his confused face.

"Uh, George, is there something wrong? And if you say nothing, I'm going to take a piece of this ice and drop it down the back of your shirt," he threatened with a grin.

Rolling her eyes, she picked up her glass and took a long drink, glaring at him as she did. How was she going to explain this to him? She took a deep breath.

"Nico, today I felt like I wasn't a partner. Like we weren't in this together." She bit her lip, trying to figure out how to continue. "I mean, telling me that *Nonno* was an organic farmer? That was a bit condescending, don't you think?"

He looked a little chagrined. "I'm sorry, George," he said softly, coming over to her.

She put her hand up. "No, don't come over here and try to George me. Today, you and Giovanni were more like partners. You hardly even acknowledged I was there."

He frowned. "*Mi dispiace.* I honestly am just not used to having a partner. May I plead that? I'm used to working mostly alone, except for Giovanni and a couple of others. When I try to explain things to my brothers, they usually get a glazed look, so I have learned not to discuss my work."

He gently put his arms around her and gave her a kiss on her cheek. "Forgive me? I'm not used to anyone caring enough to know about agricultural health or any of the topics I love."

She felt herself softening a little. "Well, I do. And these are my crops, too. I want to learn everything!"

He pulled back to look at her and, for some reason, his gaze had a wariness that made her feel uneasy. It was gone quickly, and he pulled her in for a quick hug.

"Then, partner, let's go find us some dinner and talk about our farm."

She hugged him back. Things were going to be okay. It was just a matter of getting used to each other on this new level.

twenty-one

"You're what?"

Georgie held the phone away from her ear as her father's familiar voice bellowed through her phone.

She sighed. "Daddy, you aren't hard of hearing. I said I was getting married."

"So, he finally convinced you! You're going to marry that Italian?"

Georgie frowned at his accusatory tone. "Yes, Nico is Italian, and yes, I am going to marry him," she said softly. Glancing over her shoulder, she was relieved Nico was still outside, focusing on taking soil and bark samples.

"He received half of your inheritance, and he wants the other half," her father continued. "Oh yes, your mother told me. I can't believe your grandfather did that, but then again, I never really understood your mother's family."

Georgie opened her mouth to tell him he never tried to but then closed it again. This had been a courtesy call in the last-ditch effort to reconcile with her father. Surprisingly, it had been Nico who suggested it. He had told her over dinner that he would do anything to make peace with his own father if he was still alive. Georgie knew little about Nico's father, but she guessed he was probably on a different scale than hers.

Taking a deep breath, she tried to be patient. "Daddy, I'll remind you once again that Nico doesn't need the money or the land. His family is extremely wealthy in their own right."

"Don't be naïve, Georgina," her father admonished. "His brother might be a billionaire, but that doesn't mean he is. And that land is everything. If it were mine, I'd be putting in a resort tomorrow. Sicily's becoming a major travel destination. I'd build a five-star hotel and attract people to that part of the island. I'm sure there's still nothing there—there wasn't when I visited. But if you do it right, then they'll come. In fact, that Italian has probably already thought of that."

Georgie rolled her eyes. "Daddy, his name is Nico. Please call him that! And you don't know him at all. He loves the land and would never mow down lemon groves to build some monstrosity. That's completely against everything he stands for."

She heard her father's deflated sigh. "You're not returning to London?"

"*You* aren't even living in London, Daddy," Georgie reminded him, before trying a gentler tone. "London will always be home to me. I'll be going back, but just to tie up some loose ends. We haven't sorted out all the details yet." Georgie bit her nail nervously. They really should hammer out their future soon. "But I love Nico, and I want to marry him."

"There's no changing your mind?"

"No."

He gave a small snort. "Well, the good news will be at least he will keep you away from flying."

Georgie felt her ire rising. "What makes you think that? I am always going to fly."

"If he has a brain, he will convince you not to."

It was Georgie sighing now. She quickly told her father goodbye and hung up before she said something she would regret. While she was used to his caustic remarks about her being a pilot, it was hard to hear him degrade Nico like that.

"How did it go?"

Georgie turned her head sharply to see Nico standing near the French doors to the porch wearing worn jeans, a black T-shirt and rubber boots. He couldn't have looked less like a billionaire or a resort developer if he tried. Smiling, she went to him and threw her arms around him, hugging him tightly.

"That bad, huh?" he asked, returning her hug, but keeping his hands, which were covered with dirt from touching her.

She shook her head that was buried in his chest. "It doesn't matter."

He used his hands now on her arms to gently draw her away from him. Guilty, she looked up to meet his gaze.

"But it does. If your Papa hates me, it will always drive a wedge between us."

She frowned. "I don't care what he thinks. Honestly, Nico, we're not close."

"You say that now, but it will wear on you. We must find a way for him to accept me," he said stubbornly. "Perhaps I should go and speak with him. I'm no longer the young, inexperienced man he once met. If he sees what I have become, he may relent and accept me, at least."

Georgie smiled nervously, not wanting to crush his pride. Her father was not only stubborn but a snob. He came from old money, and even though Nico and his family's wealth far surpassed most of her father's friends and acquaintances, it simply did not matter. Nico didn't have a name or the right lineage. It was better to change the subject. She glanced down at her now muddy arms. "Maybe you should wash your hands first," she teased.

Nico threw his head back and laughed and then held them toward her, wiggling his fingers. Shrieking, Georgie backed up and ran. "Not this top! I'm wearing white, Nico," she yelled. Two arms fiercely came around her in a big bear hug, and she felt his lips on her neck, moving beyond her hair that was in a ponytail. She arched her neck to give him better access, feeling his soft lips travel toward her ear. Everything seemed to float away, and nothing mattered anymore. "Well, there is a washing machine," she murmured.

twenty-two

"I am so sorry," Nico's sister-in-law Kate said anxiously. She quickly grabbed her toddler son, Frankie, and pulled his sticky hands away from Georgie's skirt. "He rarely hugs people he doesn't know. He must really like you!"

Georgie glanced down and almost laughed out loud. Tiny handprints dotted her white linen skirt she had bought earlier on a last-minute shopping trip in Positano. She and Nico had arrived by helicopter that morning, and despite his laughing protest, she told him to go find something to do while she bought some new clothes. Georgie was tired of living out of a suitcase, and Nico had seen all her clothes several times over.

"It's perfectly alright, really," Georgie rushed to reassure Nico's sister-in-law. Georgie had found her to be warm and wonderful, and obviously she and Marco were deeply in love. "He's a lot like his uncle," Georgie remarked dryly, thinking of her long-lost white shirt that she had been forced to toss. Even after using bleach, the stubborn stains refused to come out.

"He is, isn't he?" Kate said with a proud smile, not completely comprehending the meaning behind Georgie's words. "Everyone thinks Frankie looks like Marco, but I think he favors Nico—especially in personality." Kate washed the small boy's hands with wipes, setting him down to toddle on the stone porch. He kicked a nearby ball and ran off with it, his laugher musically ringing in the lemon-scented air. Georgie grinned at the memory of the excitement that had lit up the small boy's face when he saw his uncle. Frankie had spent several minutes on Nico's shoulders before pulling his uncle outside, begging him to chase him. The two had ended up rolling around the grass together, oblivious to anyone else, lost in their joy together.

Now the women were sitting out on the back veranda of the family's home, admiring the view of the vast grove before them. Georgie had met Marco and Kate immediately when they arrived. The couple spilled out the front door eagerly before Nico's car had slid to a halt. Their mother, Margherita, was up at the lemon grove's venue, hosting a large reception. After they settled in, the brothers went to join her to lend their support, but Georgie secretly knew Nico was trying to mitigate the overwhelming family scene by breaking her in with Kate. Before he left, he mentioned his other brother Stefano and his wife, Teresa, would be arriving shortly. As they waited, Georgie relaxed, instantly feeling a strong connection toward Kate, who insisted Georgie call her Katie, like the family did.

"That's a beautiful skirt. If he ruined it, I'll replace it," Kate said nervously, sitting back in her own cool pink sundress that was simply cut, but Georgie knew probably cost a fortune.

Georgie shook her head and smiled. "I'm sure it will come out. And it was a panic buy if you must know. I bought it this morning at this cute little shop in Positano."

"I thought I recognized it!" Kate exclaimed and laughed. "By any chance, did a tall, gorgeous woman with straight blonde hair sell it to you?"

"Yes, and tried to sell me half the shop with it," Georgie said and laughed. "Do you know her?"

Kate grinned. "That's our Francesca. We love her but she could sell sand in the Sahara. She was one of my first friends here. I bet she drooled when she found out you were Nico's fiancé. She adores the Rinaldi brothers. They're like family to her."

George bit her lip. "I didn't tell her. I mean, I wasn't sure who knew who, and it just never came up. I think she just assumed I was a holiday maker."

Kate looked at her, puzzled. "Where was Nico?"

"He went to visit someone named Alfonso," Georgie explained. "I guess he runs the ceramic shop."

Kate smiled, nodding. "Alfonso is family. He was the second person I met when I arrived, with Marco being the first. He's like another brother. Marco lived with Alfonso and his parents when he was younger, and his uncle was trying to teach him a few lessons. We all adore Alfonso."

Georgie took a long sip of the lemonade Kate gave her when they sat down. "I can't wait to meet him, but honestly, Katie, there's so many people. I'm an only child, so it's a bit different from what I'm used to when it comes to family."

Kate laughed. "Oh, I understand. Believe me. And you haven't seen anything yet! But I hope you'll like everyone once you get to know us. We are so happy for you, Georgie. You don't mind if I call you that, do you? Nico was so proper, introducing you so formally as *Georgina*," Kate said, drawing the name out.

Georgie grinned at Kate's impression of Nico. "Most people call me Georgie, but of course, Nico calls me George."

Kate nodded. "It all makes sense now. I was so confused at first." At Georgie's startled expression, she laughed. "He told me at Meara's wedding that he was in love with George. But he told me you were married."

Georgie looked horrified. "But I wasn't! I mean, I didn't. Goodness, you don't think..."

Kate leaned forward earnestly. "No, of course not. Marco

explained it all to me. Nico told him the minute he found out that you never got married. Marco was so happy for his little brother. He told me Nico has loved you for a very long time. It must be nice to have known him as a younger boy."

Georgie smiled, remembering the teenage version of Nico. "He was mischievous and loud. But he made me laugh harder than anyone I ever met, and to this day, I never know what he's going to do to surprise me."

A sudden wail came from the other side of the porch. Frankie had wandered into the dirt to get his ball. Apparently, he had decided to sit down and run his hands through the flower beds. The sprinklers spurted on and were spraying him intently, and he was quickly becoming a muddy mess.

Georgie winced. "He definitely favors his uncle."

GEORGIE SAT BACK and mentally went around the table, making sure she remembered the details about Nico's family members. She nervously had changed into a new green sundress after helping Katie bathe the muddy toddler. Kate explained they had a nanny, but they had left her at their villa in Rome. "I still can't get used to having one," Kate confided. "Don't get me wrong. It comes in handy when Marco and I want to have a date night. And I still have my business, so I'm grateful during the day. But for times like this, when it's just family around, I want to be with him all the time."

"Do you visit here often?" Georgie inquired.

"As much as possible," Kate confided. "Positano was my first love even before Marco. We have a villa there, but we're building one here at the lemon grove. This family loves being together," she said, clearly assessing Georgie's reaction. Georgie was careful to keep her expression neutral. She was still getting used to Nico, and now, surrounded by his family, it was almost overwhelming.

Stefano arrived a few hours before dinner with Teresa. They explained they were in Milan, working on his new pasta company before returning home to their villa in Capri. Georgie purposely avoided Nico's smirk when Teresa gave her a bearhug as a greeting. Petite and vivacious, Teresa and her cloud of black curls was the same that Georgie had seen in the photo online. Now watching Teresa dreamily gazing up at her husband, Georgie almost laughed at the thought of Teresa and Nico together.

Observing the laughing group at the table, Georgie could see the closeness. Nico explained on the way there that his family's bond was unbreakable. He wasn't sure if it was the hardship of their father leaving, the values instilled by their mother and uncle, or just the fact that they simply liked each other so much. Earlier, they devoured a delicious dinner, beginning with an extensive antipasto, followed by *Pasta alla Norma* with its silken nuggets of fried eggplant, aromatic basil, and salted ricotta. Georgie had smiled wondering if Nico had told Stefano about her eggplant obsession. Then came *braciole*, flank steak rolled with breadcrumbs and parmesan and simmered in marinara alongside garlic-infused *broccolini*. Stefano had prepared everything effortlessly, but Teresa teased Georgie. "He must really like you. He saves the *braciole* for special guests!"

Georgie savored it, remembering her grandmother's delicious version. Now enjoying wine and *cannoli*, no one seemed in a hurry to leave the table.

"Mamma, remember when Nico ran away from home for what was it? Two hours?" Stefano said with a laugh.

"And to make sure we wouldn't eat his stash of candy while he was gone, he licked it all so we wouldn't touch it. He left a note saying so," Marco added.

Nico protested, to no avail, above all the laughter. His brothers were telling every embarrassing story they could remember, and Georgie had a feeling she only heard a small portion of them.

"Georgie, you must forgive my two oldest sons," Margherita said, giving them a fierce motherly glare. "They have been waiting for this moment for many years, and apparently they need to provide you with all the details about Nico's youth in one evening."

Georgie smiled widely at her before looking up at Nico's tender grin. He had pulled her close, his arm around her. She felt the warmth of his chest, clad in a cream-colored shirt and lightweight beige pants. He looked comfortable and at peace.

"I believe it's a rite of passage," Georgie told her with a laugh. "At least that's what I heard earlier from Katie."

"You don't know the half of it," Kate remarked, giving her husband a teasing look. She and Marco had returned to the table with a baby monitor after putting Frankie to bed.

"This one brought me here with a stained shirt after practically being mauled by paparazzi," Kate told her, rolling her eyes. "Nico was here, thank God. Because then Marco took off for business, and I was at loose ends. Of course, Rita was so welcoming, but Nico and I became buddies, didn't we?"

He nodded. "I told you that you were my sister from day one. Even before you knew you would be," he said with a grin. "Katie encouraged me to get my certifications." He gave his brothers a mocking look. "She even came to my greenhouses and pretended to be interested."

"'Pretended' being the operative word," Marco said, leaning forward to put his arm on Kate's knee. She swatted him. "I was interested! Nico has a gift."

Georgie smiled, snuggling closer to Nico. "Oh, I know. My *nonno* thought so, too," she said softly.

"What about me?" Teresa interjected. "I laughed at all Nico's jokes. Even the ones that weren't funny!"

Nico chuckled. "Yes, *mia sorella*, you, too.

"Returning to my original discussion, Georgie, I hope you know how happy we are that you are here. And it's nice to renew my acquaintance with you. I am overjoyed to welcome a new daughter," Margherita said formally, but kindly.

Georgie forced a smile, but Nico's body stiffened. Was he remembering when she had come on her own to see Margherita? She nodded shyly. "Thank you, Margherita."

The older woman smiled. "Please call me, Rita, dear."

"And tomorrow more family arrives. You will need to be brave, Georgie," Marco said with a bemused expression.

Her eyes widened. "More family?"

"Well, yes, just a few, dear," Margherita said. "For the *festa* of course."

Georgie looked bewildered. Sitting up straight, she turned to Nico, who had a guilty look crossing his face. "*Festa?*"

Teresa and Kate both leaned forward, eyes alert.

"Let me guess. He didn't tell you we are hosting an engagement party for you?" Teresa said accusingly.

Katie turned and shoved Marco in his chest. "What is with you Rinaldi brothers?"

"What did I do?" Marco said, bemused, grabbing her hand and kissing it. Kate turned back toward Georgie and smiled charmingly. "Georgie, if it's okay, we would like to host an engagement party for you guys."

Georgie looked at the expectant faces. "Sure. I mean, that's fine, of course. I just didn't know." She looked again at Nico, raising an eyebrow.

He pulled her over, kissing her with a furrowed brow. "*Mi dispiace*," he murmured.

"We'll talk about this later, Nico," she said quietly.

"No, talk about it now," Stefano said, clearly egging her on. Teresa gave him a little tap on his arm, looking at him reprovingly. She turned back to Georgie with a grin. "I have a great idea. We'll leave these guys to fight their battles while we go do something a little more interesting."

"What do you have in mind?" Georgie asked tentatively.

"Just a tiny bit of shopping," Kate said, nodding.

Georgie laughed. "Now that sounds like a plan."

twenty-three

Nico puttered around his extensive greenhouse, checking the irrigation system and repotting some of his more delicate plants. Though the grove had an extensive agricultural team, he only allowed a few people in his greenhouse. Despite his meticulous instructions, some tasks were not up to his standards. This was where he liked to experiment, grafting various roses and other flowers. His mother called it playing in the dirt, which he gladly accepted.

It felt good today to be alone with his plants. He needed the silence and the space to think. So much had happened over the last month. While he loved being with Georgie, they had spent little time apart in the last few weeks, and he needed to clear his mind.

The engagement had happened quickly, and he had surprised her. Considering they had known each other for over a decade, their relationship was far from rushed. Their tumultuous past was probably behind his driving urge to close the deal. He frowned. He was becoming more like Marco than he thought. Georgie wasn't a deal. She was the most wonderful woman he had ever met and the love of his life.

If that was the case, why did he feel unsettled? Did his uneasiness stem from Georgie's mood? Once or twice, he had seen expressions cross her face that caused him concern. Admittedly, it was tiring to keep pulling out all the stops, even though it was his desire to take her to the best restaurants and hotels, and surprise her with amusing activities. He even texted Marco in the early hours one morning to ask about using the yacht. Nico couldn't help the occasional feeling of inferiority that washed over him. Standing in front of Georgie's father had been one of the most pivotal moments of his life. Afterwards, he was driven to make something of himself; something beyond money. Being the youngest in the family, it would have been easier to let Marco lead the way or follow Stefano's footsteps. But he also recognized his passion for the land and everything about it. After several late-night soul-searching talks with various family members, he took the next step and got advanced degrees. Now his own knowledge was widely sought, and his papers were shared at international conferences. He was a coveted guest speaker. Yet, why did he still feel like the kid who dug irrigation ditches on a lemon farm?

Unwinding the nearby hose, he cleaned up his potting bench. If Georgie's father could see him now in his worn jeans and rubber boots, he would for sure reiterate his disapproval. That was a big piece of his uncertainty. While Georgie insisted she and her father were not close, it still bothered him. If he was to be her husband, he wanted to be liked, or at the very least, accepted by her family.

Last night, he was filled with regret for not mentioning that his family had wanted to throw them a party. This morning, he excused himself and whispered to Katie to distract Georgie while he worked the phones and invited her mother. He appealed to Elena to call Georgie's closest friend, Mary, and ask her to spread the word to the friends Georgie would want to come. Marco's plane would pick them up the day of the party and fly them to

Naples. Mary texted him soon after, and Nico made more calls, arranging for accommodations at a nearby exclusive hotel. Georgie would be excited about having her mother and friends attending. He would make sure she knew they would have even more guests at their wedding, which they would plan together.

Wiping his hands on a towel, he wound up the hose and took one last look around before exiting. Grabbing a clipboard that was hanging on the wall, he made notes about his work.

"Of course, I'd find you here!"

Nico turned with a grin, knowing that voice anywhere. Hanging up the clipboard, he was embraced by his cousin Lucca.

"*Cugino,* I thought you and Ellie were coming tomorrow," Nico said.

Lucca grinned. "Something about a call from Katie and a shopping trip to Capri made my wife start throwing things in a suitcase last night like we were evacuating. She insisted we fly down here immediately. My security team was less than thrilled. You know Mike. He likes things perfectly planned."

Nico stared at his handsome cousin whose face was known worldwide for his roles on the big screen that included everything from a superhero to a CIA agent. He had struggled with overexuberant fans, as well as a frightening incident with a stalker who was now in prison. Lucca's security director, Mike Donnelly, was devoted to him and credited for coordinating the apprehension of Lucca's stalker. "Are you still getting threats?" Nico asked worriedly.

Lucca shook his head. "No, everything is fine. But Mike is... Let's just say old habits die hard. He still likes to be in control."

Nico fell into step with Lucca as they walked down the hill toward the storage sheds that outlined the property. He hadn't seen his cousin for a long time because of their schedules. They were more like brothers than cousins.

Lucca stared at him. "Something on your mind, Nico?" Lucca's penetrating blue eyes that he was famous for were inquisitive. Nico knew his cousin had always been good at reading his expressions. While Nico wanted to confide some of his current feelings, now wasn't the time. They would be down the hill shortly, and family would surround them.

"I am just excited you're here. I can't wait for you to meet Georgie."

Lucca slapped him on the back. "I am excited to meet your future bride, *cugino*. But I think we have some time to wait. This shopping trip sounded like a daylong adventure. How about you go get one layer of mud washed off and we'll go find Stefano and Marco? Maybe we can find something to do while they shop."

"What do you have in mind?"

Lucca grinned. "Just a friendly game."

GEORGIE GLANCED AT NICO, who was standing at the far side of the veranda, talking to Marco. He rubbed his back as he talked, grimacing. She exchanged a knowing look with Ellie, who was biting her lip, clearly trying not to laugh. Lucca hobbled over to deliver drinks to them as they sat on the porch swing, gently swaying. The family was gathering for an *aperitivo*.

"Ellie, is something amusing you?" Lucca asked, frowning.

"Nope," Ellie choked out.

"*Grazie,*" Georgie said automatically, reaching for the lemon spritzer that Lucca handed her. She took a big sip, pretending not to notice their banter. She still was in shock that she was being served a drink by one of the world's most famous actors. And then there was Ellie, whose parents were Hollywood legends. While Georgie had heard about them from Nico, it was different to actually meet them.

"If you're going to laugh," Lucca said grumpily, "then go ahead and laugh."

Ellie's laughter rang out suddenly. Putting her drink on the side table, she giggled until tears came out of her eyes. "If you could have seen how you guys looked when we drove up," she finally sputtered. "It was like you'd come from the battlefield."

"We had," Lucca said dryly. "A football battle."

He eased himself into a chair near Ellie.

"Maybe you're just getting old," Ellie said, leaning forward to rub Lucca's leg. He instantly grabbed her hand and held it over his heart. Georgie could feel the heat between the couple, who were obviously very much in love.

Lucca grimaced. "Age has nothing to do with it. I knew Alfonso had steadily improved at *calcio*. I mean, he's been advancing in the division teams, but wow. He kicked our butts."

Ellie chuckled. "I never knew soccer was such a rough sport! Sounds like our shopping trip, doesn't it, Georgie? You and I could barely keep up."

Georgie joined her laughter, but she would never complain about the day. The women had enjoyed themselves tremendously. It was like she had known Kate, Ellie, and Teresa for a long time. Joining them was Kate's friend Francesca, who had helped Georgie in the shop on her first day. At first, Georgie was intimidated by the stunning woman, who was dressed in the latest fashion, down to her spikey sandals.

"Don't worry, I felt like a frump around her the first time, too," Kate had whispered in Georgie's ear. "But Francesca is the best shopper I know, and she has a heart of gold."

Francesca embraced Georgie immediately and, as predicted, waxed on about the Rinaldi family. "You're all so fortunate. Men like that are hard to come by," Francesca said. "And Nico—he's the sweetest one," she added. Georgie expected the other women to disagree and claim their own husbands wore that title, but they all agreed. "Nico is the favorite of the family," Teresa told her while they rode on Kate and Marco's boat to Capri. "We all adore him."

"I do, too," Georgie assured her. She was grateful for the

acceptance these women were demonstrating to her, given that they obviously held high standards for who Nico would marry.

They rode the funicular up to the top, which Teresa, who was from San Francisco, laughingly described as a sideways cable car. After a leisurely lunch at a restaurant in the *Piazzetta*, they set out for an afternoon of the most glorious shopping Georgie had ever experienced. Bypassing some of the more well-known designer boutiques, Francesca led them to smaller, quaint shops. Kate was right in that Francesca was a professional shopper. With lightning speed, she darted through the rounders, snatching clothes and thrusting them at the eager saleswomen. Georgie was led into a dressing room, where she tried on an array of items with Kate's assistance. Shy at first, it was challenging to emerge and show everyone who had settled comfortably into chairs, waiting for her. Their cheers, catcalls, and laughter soon filled the store, and Georgie began to play to it. Doing her best model walk past them, they clapped and whistled. Exiting the dressing room in a cream-colored gown that left one shoulder bare, she paused and slowly turned. This time, the crowd was silent.

"You don't like it?" Georgie asked, biting her lip. "Does it look weird with my cast?"

"Not at all. You look stunning," Kate whispered.

"Perfect," Ellie agreed.

"*Perfetto*," Francesca reiterated.

"I love that you have kinky hair like me," Teresa said, blindly off-topic, reaching a hand into her bag of chips. That made the entire group laugh.

The dress had been deemed just right for the engagement party, and Georgie left the store with multiple purchases that would be magically delivered later.

"I know it's hard to get used to," Kate said, taking her arm. "It's weird having people just do things for you. At first, I felt like a fish out of water. But then again, you grew up a little differently from me."

Georgie remained quiet, not sure how to respond. Over lunch, she had shared some information about her youth. The women's questions were put innocently. They simply wanted to know more about her. Eventually, Teresa couldn't help but ask if she personally knew any members of the royal family, which caused the entire group to burst into laughter.

"Well, yes, but they are just people like us." Georgie nudged Ellie. "You know about that more than anyone here."

Ellie agreed. "Oh my God, yes. First my parents. Then believe me, if half of the female population could see what a dork Lucca is sometimes, they'd realize he's just human." She stopped and grinned. "But I have to say I'm glad he's my dork."

Now, sitting on the veranda, Georgie blinked as Nico waved his hand at her. "Hey, George, wake up. You look more exhausted than I do, and I ran about twenty miles today trying to catch up to Alfonso!"

He quickly leaned over and kissed her forehead, and she grinned up at him. "Sorry, I was just thinking about our shopping trip."

He smiled gently down at her, helping her stand. "I want to hear all about it. But right now, Mamma is waving us in for dinner." Hugging her, he whispered, "Sorry in advance."

She pulled away. "For what?"

He grinned. "You'll see."

AFTER A RAUCOUS DINNER filled with laughter and lots of teasing, Georgie better understood Nico's previous apology. It was obvious he was the instigator, telling jokes about his brothers and cousin, needling them and making them all laugh until their sides hurt. Alfonso occasionally joined in with Nico, and the two of them were the ultimate little brothers.

It was all lively fun, and Georgie loved it while also admiring her future mother-in-law. Margherita gently shepherded everyone with ease that was fun to observe. She nudged the men to go clean up the kitchen while she relaxed on the back veranda with the other women. It was then that Margherita told Georgie a sweet story about Nico as a kid, bringing her flowers all the time.

"Things were different then," Margherita said wistfully. "I worked hard, and some days were tough. Nico always sensed it, and I would find flowers at my bedside on the table and spread around the house." She laughed at the memory. "Then come to discover he was taking the roses from our special garden that we use to provide flowers for events. The gardeners began chasing him with a hose and blocked him from coming in. So then he went to the fields and picked wildflowers for me. I told him it wasn't necessary, but I looked forward to those flowers. I still do."

Georgie smiled at the story, thinking back to the times Nico had brought her flowers as well. She realized it had started at such a small age. "He brings flowers when you need them the most," she said softly.

"Not just flowers," Margherita reminisced. "When he was young, I was sick in bed. He brought me the most enormous *panino*. Of course, I couldn't eat it, and I wondered why he looked so crushed. I found out later there was a commercial on television he had seen where the child brings his mother a *panino* and she instantly springs out of bed full of energy."

Georgie reflected on that as she now strolled through the lemon grove alone with Nico after Margherita's insistence that they needed some privacy.

"You are awfully quiet," Nico remarked, and Georgie smiled a little.

"I love your family," she said softly.

Nico smiled gently at her. "They were savages at dinner. I didn't think they had any more embarrassing stories about me, but I guess they did."

Georgie laughed. "You started it! They had to defend themselves. I thought there was going to be a food fight any minute!"

"No, we're still too scared of Mamma!" He laughed before staring at her. "They're soon to be your family, too. And you will find we adopt people along the way. Alfonso, Francesca and others. Meara and Alec are coming tomorrow for our *festa*."

"I can't wait to meet them, but Meara sounds a bit intense," Georgie said nervously. "I heard stories today about her taking charge when Katie was about to give birth to Frankie."

"Oh, she did! And that doesn't really come close to describing her. You'll love her, though. She has a very kind heart."

Nico stopped walking and nestled Georgie's back against a tree. His eyes glinted in the dusk, and with both his hands, he combed through her hair on either side of her face. "Let's talk about something else," he suggested huskily in her ear.

"Hmm, politics?" she asked, as his smooth lips moved along her jawline.

"Nope," he said, as his lips grazed toward her lips.

"The state of the crops?"

"No," he whispered, intentionally keeping his lips just a centimeter from hers.

"What?" she whispered, her heart racing.

"Us," he said, swooping into claim her lips in a heated kiss that went on and on.

When he finally raised his head, Georgie sagged next to the tree. Threading her arm around his neck, she pulled his head closer again. "I have a better idea. Maybe we just don't talk for bit."

She was rewarded with the kiss of a lifetime.

twenty-four

Georgie took a sip of her tea and admired the view from the veranda over the lemon grove. Remarkably, there was a stillness around her, except the occasional bark of Lucca and Ellie's dog Sophia, who was romping in the nearby field.

She had slept in and after coming downstairs, she found everyone had gone different directions. Kate was at their villa in Positano, recording a podcast about Italy, while Lucca and Ellie had gone to scout a location site for an episode of Lucca's new television show featuring Stefano as a food expert.

Margherita told her to help herself to a cup of tea, explaining Nico was up in the greenhouse and Marco was working in the study. Stefano and Teresa were up at the venue discussing the menu for the *festa*. The prior evening, Georgie offered to help with the *festa*, but Margherita wouldn't hear of it. "Relax and enjoy a little solitude," she said before leaving to go up the hill.

Georgie frowned. The solitude wasn't something she was seeking. Just weeks ago, she would have been happy on her own. Now she was aware of every noise, Sophia's barking, a bee buzzing in the colorful Italian planter near her. Silence gave her time to think, and Georgie knew deep down that was not something she wanted to do. Suddenly, a wave of grief washed over her. She had been so busy soaking in her new life with Nico that she had pushed her sadness over her grandfather's death deep down. *Nonno* would want her to be happy, but she was still adjusting to the loss.

Looking up at the sky, she wished she was soaring in the endless blue skies. Resignedly, she went to retrieve her computer. It was probably time she checked in with her boss to see what her schedule over the next month looked like after her cast was removed and her arm was healed. She couldn't expect the other pilots to fill in for her indefinitely. Her future was uncertain, and she and Nico would need to discuss it after the *festa*.

After getting her laptop from its case, Georgie ran back down the stairs and went through the grand living room toward the back of the house. Nico gave her a tour of the house their first night, and she had glimpsed Marco's study. She would ask him for the Wi-Fi password.

As she neared the double doors, which were ajar, Nico's voice floated out. He must have returned from the greenhouse. Smiling, she approached the door when he said her name, and she stopped in her tracks. Eavesdropping wasn't her style, but something made her pause before announcing her presence.

"Georgie will understand. I'll need to explain it delicately, but eventually she'll see it's the best course," Nico said confidently. His voice carried, and she shrunk back. He must be near the door.

She heard a murmur and couldn't make out what Marco said.

Nico continued. "Of course, it's her grandfather's land, and she's attached to it. But she'll have to see that folding it into Oro Industries is the best solution."

Georgie automatically leaned forward. Oro was going to buy the property? Nico had never suggested that! That would be a cold day in hell when they would buy her property. It was *Nonno*'s legacy!

Marco mumbled something indecipherable, and laughing commenced.

"No, she has no clue," Nico said. More laughter. "Certainly, I could have told her, but it's better this way."

Marco was talking again. Blast it, she couldn't hear him. She was practically leaning against the door, and Nico's voice was near. "She'll understand," he said in a smug tone. "And she will be happy once it starts and will forget it was a secret."

That was enough. Georgie pushed the door open. She felt her face flush with anger.

"Exactly what will I be happy about?"

Nico was standing in front of Marco's desk, wearing his usual faded T-shirt and jeans. He turned to see her, his face registering surprise. Marco was sitting behind the desk, but he stood quickly, his gaze sweeping over the two of them.

"*Buongiorno*, Georgina," Marco said formally. Dressed in black slacks and a button-down collared white shirt with a striped tie, he suddenly seemed like the family patriarch to her. She had never really registered that. He was the leader of Oro, and Nico was his youngest brother. Nico would do anything to please him. And now that meant taking her land!

Georgie's eyes narrowed, but she bit back a rude reply, choosing to take a deep breath instead. Nico walked toward her, his eyes searching her face. "George, we were just talking."

"I heard you," she stated flatly.

Marco grabbed his suit jacket that had been slung over his leather office chair. Shrugging it on, he smiled gently at Georgie. "I'll leave you two to talk. I have a meeting close to here, and then I told Katie I'd be home for lunch. We'll see you both tomorrow for the *festa*," he said. As he walked by, he put a hand on Nico's shoulder, and in that paternal movement, Georgie's mind raced with clarity. It was almost a signal that he was in charge.

Nico stared at her intently. "Georgie, I don't know what you heard but sit down. Let's talk."

She frowned. "If it's about taking my land, then we are most certainly NOT talking about it! I know I might seem very *understanding*"—she emphasized the last word—"but guess what? That's not happening," she said, poking him in the chest.

"George…"

"Oh, for heaven's sake, don't George me," she almost shouted. "You think you're going to take *Nonno*'s land? My father was right!"

"Your father was right?" he asked sarcastically. "That's rich. Just a few days ago, you were telling me that his opinion meant nothing."

"It does when he's right!" she shouted.

Nico glared at her. "I don't know what you think you heard, but you're way off. If you would calm down for a second, I will explain."

Unexpectedly, every repressed feeling bubbled to the surface. Anger at her grandfather's death, his ridiculous will, and now this betrayal. Then there was Nico's unfamiliar behavior, wanting to impress her, and finally, the rushed engagement. It all made sense now. Undoubtedly, he loved her, but he also wanted her to fall in line with his plans. She exhaled slowly and stared at him.

He was clearly growing angry but was trying to stay calm. His usual warm eyes glinted at her, and his mouth was a firm line. "I was going to talk to you all about this," he began.

"When?" she interrupted. "Before or after our wedding?"

"What does our wedding have to do with anything?" he asked roughly.

"Seems to me you wanted to rush to the altar for another reason," she answered.

"What does that mean?"

"What it sounds like! Are you even in love with me, or was that a play to get the land? Marry me and then fold it into your family's company? I can't believe I didn't see this coming!"

"You are questioning my love for you?" He asked so quietly, it sent a shiver down her spine.

They stared at each other for a few seconds. She watched as the muscle in his cheek twitched. He was trying to control his fury.

"This is all a misunderstanding," he said, using a calmer tone. "Marco and I were talking about a few things. If you would just let me explain—"

"I don't want you to explain! I already get it. Your brother's the one in charge, isn't he? He's the one who came up with this entire plan, and you're just going along with it as the youngest. It's like you're one of the *pupi* we saw a few weeks ago. You once told me you had a hard time saying no to Marco."

"That's when I was younger, Georgie! I have told Marco no many times, especially over the course of the last year. I have resigned most of my duties at Oro to pursue my passion. You know that! Marco and I were just talking about—"

"It doesn't matter anymore, Nico," she said dully. "Sharing the property with you was a mistake! You don't want me involved, admit it! That day with Giovanni, you didn't care at all what I thought!"

"I apologized for that, Georgie."

"Perhaps this shouldn't happen between us," Georgie said, not meeting his gaze. She twisted her ring around her finger nervously.

"Georgie! What are you saying? *Per favore*!" He ran his hands through his hair. "Don't do this again!"

Her eyes narrowed. "*Again*?"

"Yes, again. You left me once, and now you're doing it once more. It's almost like you want an excuse. You won't listen to what I have to say. Are you looking for a reason? Or is it just that you don't trust me?" he finished sadly.

"Trust? That's interesting. Yet, you're the one dragging up ancient history. I thought we were past that, but you're always going to throw it in my face, aren't you? You say we have healed old wounds, but it's clearly not true. I thought we'd moved on."

He looked stunned. "We have come far. We're partners!"

"Well, partner," she drawled. "I quit." Taking her engagement ring off, she set it roughly down on the desk. It swirled roughly for a moment before stopping to lie still. They both stared at it, almost in shock.

She finally spoke. "Goodbye, Nico, *again.*"

twenty-five

Georgie dug her chopsticks into the carton of chicken pad Thai and took another unenthusiastic bite. Back in England for the last three weeks, she still didn't have much of an appetite, and she deliberately chose food that didn't resemble the flavors of Italian cuisine.

At first, her flat was her refuge. Now it was turning into her prison. Even her glorious view overlooking St. Regent's Park did nothing to cheer her. As the lights slowly flickered on at dusk, she longed to be enjoying the view of the lemon grove with its sweet scent. Every night, she promised she would begin the next day differently, and move forward with her life.

Throwing the chopsticks back in the carton with despair, she sat back. Flexing her left arm, she did a slow stretch with it. Last week she had the cast removed and almost didn't recognize the pale, atrophied limb. The doctor told her it would build back soon enough, and the physical therapist had shown her what exercises and light weights to use. For now, it looked a little scrawny next to her other arm, but at least she was rid of the cast.

Georgie's phone buzzed next to her, and she ignored it. Rather than even see who it was, she just turned it over and stubbornly set it on the table next to her. She might as well turn it off. It was probably her mother again.

When Georgie arrived back in London, she had reluctantly called Elena. It was better to just get it over with quickly and tell her that she and Nico had parted ways. Her mother had sounded more startled than Georgie expected. Hesitantly, Elena told her that she was not in England, but in Italy. Marco's plane had just landed in Naples, carrying Elena, Mary, and other friends. Georgie was mortified.

"I had no idea, Mum."

"It was to be a surprise," Elena said dryly. Practical as always, she begged off to go spread the word among the travelers. Mary texted shortly after, asking her if she was okay and explaining that they were going to spend the night before traveling home on Marco's plane. Upon returning, her mother phoned often, but also seemed to sense Georgie needed space. In return, Georgie reassured her, usually by text, that she was fine.

After politely answering Mary and her other friends' texts, she kept to herself. Checking in with her boss, Georgie used her arm as a convenient excuse to put off flying for a few more weeks. "I thought we might lose you to Sicily," he said cheerfully. Georgie had choked back a sob and assured him that no, she was still living in London.

Georgie's phone buzzed again, interrupting her thoughts. She ignored it. Undoubtedly, it would be Mary this time. She should probably return her calls, but her friend would ask questions she wasn't ready to answer. Texts were safer. Georgie wasn't ready for her emotions to come out. Holding them tightly inside was easier.

Knocking commenced at her door. Who could that be? Another resident in the building? Everyone else had to go through the security desk. Not even caring anymore, she opened the door, and Mary stood in the hallway holding a white bag with a furious expression. "I just came over to tell you I resign as your best friend," she announced as she swept into the flat, casting aside her coat. Petite with short brown hair, Mary looked sweet but was in fact, fiery and direct. It's what had endeared Georgie to her early on in school.

Now with Mary staring at her, finally, the dam broke. The next thing she knew, Georgie was sobbing into Mary's shoulder. When Georgie finally pulled away, she gave her long-time friend a watery smile. "I'm so sorry. I just knew if I saw you, that would happen."

"It is alright to cry, Georgie."

Mary held up a white paper bag. "Do you know how many blocks I had to walk with melting ice cream? And then you left me downstairs for ten minutes before I convinced your porter I wasn't going to murder you. We better eat now."

Georgie smiled again. "I don't want any ice cream but thank you."

Mary was already delving into the bag. "Silly! I didn't just bring you ice cream! I brought your favorite—sticky toffee pudding!"

Georgie picked up the fork Mary had dug out of the drawer and took a small bite to please her friend. Putting the fork down, Georgie smiled a little.

"Is that it? What kind of jilted woman are you? Looks like I'll have to eat alone."

"I wasn't jilted," Georgie remarked, walking over to sit cross-legged on the chintz-covered window seat overlooking the park.

Mary's mouth fell open. "Are you telling me you've dumped that gorgeous man again?"

"Why does everyone keep saying again?" Georgie grumbled, grabbing a throw pillow and thumping it.

Mary sat down on the comfortable sofa opposite her. Mary's eyes widened. She carefully put the carton of pudding down on the table and stared at Georgie.

"Georgina, it's me. You can tell me."

Georgie took a deep breath. Suddenly, the feelings were raw. "It started when he kissed me," she said softly.

"Which time?" Mary said dryly, licking her fork and setting it down in the carton.

Georgie laughed for the first time in days. "I guess you're right. It all started when I was sixteen."

∽

"AND THEN YOU JUST LEFT?"

"What was I supposed to do?" Georgie asked tearfully. "He and Marco were plotting to steal my land! *Nonno*'s legacy."

Mary leaned back against the cushions. Her tone was suspicious. "You're sure that's what you heard?"

"Yes!" Georgie insisted. "I told you the entire conversation."

"Georgie," Mary said quietly. "You do realize that Nico was keeping a secret?"

"Of course I do! I just told you!"

Mary leaned forward, staring intently at Georgie. "*We* were the secret—your mum, me, and about ten of your closest friends. Nico wanted to surprise you. He pulled out all the stops. We had welcome gifts waiting for us at this amazing hotel, and anything we wanted brought to us. It was like he thought of everything. Except there was no bride."

Georgie felt a sense of dread start deep down in the pit of her stomach. "You don't think that's the secret he was talking about, do you?"

Mary shrugged. "It could be. But we'll never know, will we? Because you wouldn't even let him explain."

Georgie felt fresh tears run down her cheeks. She angrily wiped them. "I heard enough. Whether he was also talking about all of you, it doesn't change the fact that he wanted my land."

Mary sighed, clearly frustrated.

Georgie glanced at her sadly. "Did you see him?"

"No. When we couldn't reach you, we tried calling Nico, but it went to voicemail. Finally, your mum remembered she had Margherita's number, from when she called to welcome her to the family."

"I didn't know about that," Georgie whispered.

"Margherita told your mum. And then she said she would have Marco arrange for our return. We didn't see anyone."

"I was on a plane headed to England. That's why I didn't answer my phone," Georgie commented thoughtfully. "I don't know where Nico was."

Mary nodded. "Margherita didn't say either. Your mum said she was kind given the circumstances, but distant."

Georgie swallowed back her emotion. Suddenly, she missed all of them, from Margherita to the other women who had been so kind and befriended her.

"What happens now?" Mary asked.

Georgie tore at a tissue distractedly. "I'm not sure. I need to sort out my life. I suppose part of me still hoped that Nico would come and tell me everything I heard wasn't true."

"Perhaps it wasn't."

"If it wasn't, he would have told me by now!" Georgie insisted.

"Is there anything I can do?"

Georgie shook her head and smiled sadly. "I'm sorry I shut you out. It's time I got on with my life. I'll contact my parents' solicitor this week. I suppose we'll have to sort out what happens with *Nonno's* land legally."

Mary stood. "It's getting late, and I have to work tomorrow." She sighed. "It's time to pull yourself together. Keep a stiff upper lip and all that," she said, patting Georgie's shoulder. "I will pop in tomorrow."

"That isn't necessary," Georgie said.

"Sure, it is. I have pudding to finish."

<h1 style="text-align:center">twenty-six</h1>

Georgie sat back at her desk, rubbing her neck. Catching up on some online training was a great way to start working before actually flying again. Its complexity forced her to keep her mind off things. Twisting in her chair, she looked out her window at the rainy day. The fog was rolling in across the park.

Her phone buzzed, and it was the security desk. Answering it, Andrew, her favorite porter, told her she had a delivery.

"Just take it for me, will you?" Georgie asked, about to hang up.

"Miss Georgie, he says you have to sign for it."

Reluctantly, Georgie told him to send the delivery person up. She went to answer her door and watched the delivery man walk down the hallway from the elevator. Thrusting an envelope at her, he handed her an electronic tablet. "Sign here, Miss," he ordered gruffly.

Tucking the envelope under her arm, she signed automatically with her finger and watched him retreat quickly, already on to the next delivery. Closing the door, she tore the envelope. It must be from the office. Taking out a sheaf of papers, a small envelope drifted to the floor. Georgie bent down to pick it up and saw the writing on it: *George*. Her heart catapulted to her feet. It was from Nico.

Georgie slid open the envelope with a nail and withdrew the small card. It contained only two lines:

"For you, George. Forever yours, Nico."

Picking up the papers, she tried to read them but had to wipe the tears from her eyes several times. Sitting down absentmindedly, she quickly scanned it a few times. It became obvious that he was selling her his share of the farm. According to the terms, she owed him one euro. She realized legally he had to ask for a sum, as he couldn't just give it to her per the will's requirements. The last sheet written by Nico's solicitor explained she must sign them in the presence of her own solicitor at her earliest convenience. He would take care of filing them in Italy. It was all done with efficiency and grace. She wouldn't expect anything less.

Sitting back, her mind raced. Her grandfather's legacy was intact. That had been what she wanted. Except she wanted Nico, too. She thought back to the aging groves, the ideas that Nico and Giovanni had discussed to regenerate them. They always honored the land. And now she would have to figure out how to.

Suddenly, Georgie wanted to talk to her mother. Pulling her phone out of her pocket, she tapped the screen, and her mother answered distractedly. "Hello, my love. I am sorry I have been so busy. How are you getting on?"

After reassuring her mother confidently that she was okay, Georgie bit her nail. "Mum, what do you think *Nonno* would want me to do with his legacy?"

"I'm confused, dear. You are *Nonno*'s legacy."

Georgie frowned. "No mum, I mean the land."

"The land wasn't his legacy."

"It was, Mum. It meant everything to him. And now...well, now Nico has sold me his share. It is all mine. Mum, I don't know what to do."

She heard her mother sigh. "I'll be right over."

IT WAS ONLY thirty minutes later when Georgie opened the door to her mother. Taking Elena's Burberry trench coat, she automatically hung it in the closet and walked into the living area to join her.

"Can I get you something to drink?" Georgie asked politely.

"Tea would be lovely," Elena responded.

After brewing the tea and bringing it to her mother, Georgie sat down on the window seat. She avoided Elena's scrutinizing gaze, knowing her mother probably guessed by her worn jeans and cozy sweatshirt that she was still avoiding the world.

"Georgina Anne, have you even left your flat? You look so pale."

Frowning, Georgie assured her mother she was fine and had been working all day. She didn't admit she hadn't even flown yet. "You didn't have to rush over."

Her mother's shoulders drooped. "I did. It was time we had this talk. I admit I made so many mistakes over the years, and I will live with those regrets. But I can't let you take on this burden by yourself."

"What burden?"

"The land, Georgie. Why did Nico just give it to you?"

"He didn't give it to me. He sold it to me for one euro," Georgie said dryly.

Elena's pursed lips demonstrated she wasn't impressed with her quip. Georgie shrugged in response to her mother's narrowed gaze. "I don't know. I guess in the end, he decided it should have been mine all along. *Nonno* was wrong to split it between us."

"Georgina, I do not believe he was," Elena said, stirring her tea. She tentatively took a sip. Placing her cup down, she smiled a little.

"I sadly learned a hard lesson with my mother's passing," she said. "My parents always seemed like they would live to be 100. On top of that, I somehow convinced myself that they didn't really want to see me after the way I treated them. They poured their love into you. But after my mother died, I was determined to build a relationship with my father. It was difficult at first. We're both stubborn Italians," she said, laughing a little.

"I didn't know you were in touch with him that much," Georgie remarked softly.

"It was something I had to do myself. I didn't want to bring you into it," her mother said. "At first, I just called, but that stubborn old man would only grunt into the phone. So, I finally flew down there. We spent a week together. I think we made a lot of progress that week, but I still had so many regrets. I think he forgave me, but I couldn't forgive myself."

Georgie stood and went over to the couch. She sat and put her arm around her mother for a minute. Reaching behind her, she grabbed a tissue and gave it to her mother.

"Oh, your arm. It's better now?" Elena remarked, dabbing at her eyes.

"Yes, it's back good as new," Georgie said. "Mum, what did *Nonno* tell you about the land?"

"He told me that though the land had been in our family for centuries, it was a responsibility he didn't want you to have to face, Georgie. He felt that commitment so deeply that it was almost a burden. He understood Nico's ideas for regenerative farming were needed. But he also admitted it would be beyond his capability to learn."

"So he decided he would give it to both me and Nico," Georgie said softly.

"That's why I was so angry when you told me," Elena said.

"You see, I thought he had decided to give the entire plot to Nico. I didn't care. Good riddance!"

"Why do you say that?" Georgie asked, confused.

"Because I saw the toll it took. And I know you! You might look like your father, but you've got my blood—my parents' blood running through your veins. I knew you'd take this gift of the land and do everything you could to honor your grandfather's wishes. He knew it, too. In the end, I think that's why he made the decision he did—to let Nico run it but share it with you, so it would still stay in the family. He couldn't quite let go of that idea. But he didn't want to burden you. He knew you had your own life. You couldn't just drop everything to properly care for a lemon farm in Sicily."

Georgie leaned her head back against the window, lost in thought.

"Mum, do you think he was also playing matchmaker? Did he want me and Nico to get back together?"

A slow smile grew on her mother's face. "Of course he did, that old fool. He adored you, and he loved that young man."

Georgie exhaled slowly. "I messed up, Mum. I accused Nico of trying to steal the land from me. I overheard a conversation with Marco and I'm still not sure what they were discussing, but it sounded like they were plotting to bring the land under the Oro Industries umbrella."

"I can't believe that Nico would do that! He loves you too much to hurt you. Did you ask him to explain?"

Georgie hung her head. "No. He tried, but I wouldn't let him. I just broke it off with him then and there."

"Georgina," her mother scolded. "You need to at least give him an opportunity."

"It's over. He sent me the papers already."

"But obviously, he still loves you."

Georgie sighed. "Yes, I believe so. I mean, I know he does.

But given our past, I'm not sure we can overcome it all. I doubt he'll ever fully trust me again."

"You won't know until you ask," Elena said.

twenty-seven

Georgie sat up straight in an uncomfortable chair in the solicitor's office. She waited patiently in the lobby for Mr. Randle's secretary to announce her arrival. Shifting the portfolio that was in her lap, she glanced inside nervously to ensure she had all the paperwork. After calling Nico repeatedly for the past week, she finally gave up and rationalized that this was what he wanted. It seemed that it was her only choice to sign the papers and send him one euro. At times, her rebellious side wanted to add several zeroes to the check and pay him what the land was truly worth. Yet they both knew it wasn't about money. It never was.

A buzzing came from her purse, and Georgie reached inside for her phone. Whoever it was would have to wait until this appointment was over. Mr. Randle had fit her in as a favor, and she hoped he hadn't told her father. Georgie still hadn't spoken to him since she returned from Italy, as she wasn't up to hearing him gloat over her breakup with Nico. If she told him that now she solely owned a vast number of hectares in Italy, he would strongly urge her to sell it. While she had no idea yet what her future plans were, she would at least set the wheels in motion legally and have that conversation later.

Finally locating her phone, her heart somersaulted as she saw Marco's name appear. Her finger hovered over the answer button until she finally swallowed hard and pressed it. He was probably calling to inquire about buying the land. This was her opportunity to strongly tell him in no uncertain terms it was not for sale.

"*Ciao*, Marco," she said coolly.

"Georgina." Marco's voice sounded frantic. "There's been an accident."

"What kind of accident?" she asked sharply.

"A brush fire. It spread quickly. Your *nonni's* house caught on fire."

"Oh, my God! No!"

Georgie stood abruptly, the portfolio crashing to the floor. The receptionist in the quiet office raised her head sharply. Georgie picked up her portfolio and opened the door to the hallway. "Please tell me it's okay," she pleaded, taking a deep breath.

"It's not okay," said Marco grimly. He was breathing hard. "And neither is my brother!"

"Nico? Oh God, Marco. He is alright, though, isn't he?"

"We don't know yet. He ran into your *nonni's* home!" said Marco roughly. "*Stupido*! My brother. And as he was exiting the house, a beam fell on him. We were fortunate that the fire brigade had just arrived, and they dragged him out. He's at the hospital in Palermo in *Terapia Intensiva.*"

"Intensive Care?" Georgie automatically translated. "But he will be fine?" Her heart was racing. She grabbed onto the wall in the hallway to steady herself.

"We don't know yet," Marco said firmly. "I just thought you ought to know about your *nonni's* home."

"I don't care about that now. I care about Nico."

She heard him make a sound of disbelief. "You could have fooled me."

~

GEORGIE FELT UNBELIEVABLY AWKWARD. She arrived at the Palermo hospital just hours after Marco's call. Stopping at her flat to throw random clothes in a bag, she quickly donned the first things she found, jeans and a top. On her way to the private airport in Central London in a hired car, she realized with a sinking heart that she was in no shape to fly. Fate intervened when she arrived, as she collided with a former instructor who agreed to fly her to Palermo. Georgie would be forever grateful.

It was only while she was in the taxi to the hospital that she glanced down and saw she had dragged on a T-shirt that Nico once bought her as a joke. I 🤍 *Sicily* was blazoned across her chest like she was a holiday maker. Her hair, once straight and styled, had rebelled to its normal corkscrews. After being directed to the unit Nico was in, she ran down the hall only to stop short at the waiting area. With her usual clumsiness, she overshot it and fell in a heap in front of Nico's family. When everyone rose quickly, she scrambled to her feet. There was no way she would suffer the indignity of them helping her stand.

With their stony faces, who knew if they would have even offered? Marco and Kate were there, as well as were Stefano and Teresa. Lucca and Ellie sat in the corner. A tall red-haired woman who was sitting with Kate turned and gave her a narrowed gaze. Likely, she was Kate's sister, Meara. Georgie glanced around for Margherita, who she knew would be civil even if she wasn't necessarily an ally.

"Georgie, we didn't expect you," Kate said, glancing nervously at her husband. Marco stared at Georgie with eyes that glinted like steel, and a shiver chased up her spine.

"I had to come," Georgie answered softly.

"We are pleased you are here," came a voice from behind her. Georgie turned to see Margherita. The older woman looked like she had aged ten years since Georgie had last seen her.

"Oh, Rita," Georgie said, spontaneously and uncharacteristically throwing her arms around her. Georgie was relieved when Margherita hugged her back. Eventually, the older woman pulled back and eyed Georgie steadily. "I just came from Nico's bedside."

"How is he?" Marco asked abruptly, stepping forward.

"He's doing as well as expected," said a masculine voice. Georgie looked behind Margherita at the handsome doctor, who was wearing green scrubs. He had a mass of dark hair and big, thick black glasses. Meara, who had stood, now hastened to come forward and put her arm through his.

Always polite, Margherita turned to Georgie. "Georgie, this is Doctor Alessandro Amato, Meara's husband. Oh, you probably also haven't met Meara, Katie's sister."

After awkward nods, Margherita continued. "Though this is not Alec's specialty, he has been helping navigate Nico's medical needs."

The group moved in closer, waiting for him to speak.

"They are prepping him for surgery. Nico was very fortunate," Alec explained gravely. "The part of the beam that hit him was not engulfed in flames. Nico has some internal injuries and a broken leg. Thankfully, we don't believe he suffered any head injuries. He has some minor burns on one hand. Otherwise, he was not burned, but he suffered smoke inhalation. When I heard it was a fire, of course, I thought he would require treatment in a burn unit."

Marco was the first to speak. "Alec, what kind of operation? I want all the best medical care. Tell me who to fly in. We will get whoever we need!"

Alec smiled, reaching out to lay a hand on Marco's shoulder.

"He's receiving extraordinary care, Marco. There isn't time. They have done imaging tests, and it looks like he could lose his spleen. They also want to make sure there's no internal bleeding. They'll handle the leg later if you want your own orthopedic doctor to fly in."

"I do," Marco said firmly. "I'll call him now." He turned, running a hand through his hair. "*Stupido*! I cannot believe he ran into a burning house." He turned to glare at Georgie. "All to please you! The land wasn't enough. He had to sacrifice himself to save mementos for you!"

Kate looked helpless. Wiping away tears, she grabbed her husband's arm to comfort him. Margherita moved in front of Georgie, almost acting as a shield. "*Basta*! Enough!" Her sweeping gaze took in all of them. "Georgie is our guest. You will treat her as such! Marco, I raised you better than this! I don't care how upset you are!"

"Mamma," he said, his eyes filling with tears. "It's Nico."

"That is no excuse," she said, her lips firm. "Apologize to Georgie right now. And if one more cruel word is spoken, I will take care of you!"

Lucca made a sound that almost sounded like a snicker and was quelled by a look from Ellie.

Georgie rushed to speak. "Rita, thank you, but I understand. Everyone is just worried, and I know I am probably the last person they want to see."

"*Mi dispiace*," Marco ground out. "Please accept my apology on behalf of myself and my family. Katie, I need some air. *Per favore*. Let's go for a walk." Marco grabbed Kate's hand and tugged her down the hall. The others drifted away into different directions and Georgie turned, walking over to the corner of the room to look out the window. Taking big gulps, she tried not to sob. Internal injuries? What did that mean? Why did he run into the burning house? How could he be so reckless?

A tentative arm reached across her back, and Georgie turned

to Teresa's concerned gaze. "If it helps, I used to be a nurse. Well, I guess I am still a nurse. One day, I'll return to nursing," she said. "I know it sounds bad, but I have seen worse. Right now, you look like you need to sit down."

Pushing Georgie gently into the chair, Teresa disappeared and came back with a cup. "Drink some orange juice," she said. "Trust me, you want to avoid the coffee here, but I think you should raise your blood sugar a little." She made a face. "I usually have some candy for a time like this, but I ate what was in my purse while we were waiting and I haven't had a chance to find the vending machines."

Georgie smiled a little. Teresa, widely known for her junk food habits, was so kind. "Thank you," she said quietly, glancing quickly behind her to see who was around. Seemingly reading her thoughts, Teresa rushed to reassure her. "Stefano took Rita to the chapel. The others have gone to the cafeteria."

"I just don't want you to get in trouble for being nice to me," Georgie remarked sadly. "I have been such an idiot, Teresa."

"Well, first of all, I always do what I want. Ellie and Katie would be here, too, if they didn't have to calm their husbands down first." She rolled her eyes. "These hot-headed Italians."

Georgie sadly stared into the cup of orange juice. "I can understand, though. They must think I am a terrible person. Running out after everyone had done so much for our engagement party."

"Well, yes, that wasn't your finest moment, but we knew there had to be more to the story," Teresa said, staring at her with a small smile. "Listen, I'm not here to judge you. I know you love Nico. I saw with my own eyes how much. It takes two to screw up a relationship, so I know Nico had a part in this."

Georgie wiped her eyes with her hand roughly. "I honestly don't even know anymore. I'm so confused!"

Teresa nodded sympathetically. "These Rinaldi men are a

mass of contradictions. I am still figuring it all out. And you and Nico will figure it out, too."

"It's too late," Georgie said miserably. "He probably hates me."

"Oh, for God's sake, pull it together!" Both Georgie and Teresa jumped at the voice behind them. Meara was standing before them looking like she just left the boardroom, wearing a perfectly pressed black suit with an emerald green silk blouse. Georgie flushed, glancing down at her casual clothes.

"Um, this is Meara," said Teresa, biting her lip, with humor in her eyes. "I apologize in advance for anything she says."

Meara gave Teresa a dark look.

"Stuff it, Rossi."

Teresa grinned. "It's Rinaldi now Meara."

Meara smirked before cooly assessing Georgie. "Georgie, despite your questionable taste in T-shirts, I know you have a brain. Of course, I took a few minutes to cyberstalk you, being that you were going to marry our Nico. Once I got past the photos of your clubbing days and your uh, unfortunate almost wedding, I saw your company's website. I think it's admirable what you do—flying medical teams around the world. You're obviously a very skilled pilot. And Teresa will tell you I don't give compliments lightly."

At Teresa's snort, Meara continued. "In fact, I was told you're a little like me. Independent with a tough exterior," Meara said with a smirk. "But of course, a heart of gold." She glanced at Teresa as if defying her to disagree. "But what are you doing here, shrinking in the corner? Don't let them intimidate you," Meara continued. "A man who runs into a burning house to save something for the woman he loves wants to be with her. Just my educated guess. You have every right to be here, and when Nico comes to, eventually, he will see that as well. Where's your British phlegm, girl?"

Georgie felt laughter bubble up. Teresa was the first to ask,

"Meara, what do you know about British phlegm? And what is that exactly? It sounds disgusting."

Meara shrugged. "I heard it in an old movie or somewhere. All I know is you should be made of stronger stock, Georgie. English and Italian? That is a stern combination."

Georgie stood, smiling a little. "You're right, even though strong is not the word I'd use to describe me right now." She reached over and gave her a small hug. Meara visibly stiffened. "Oh God, not another hugger in the family!"

twenty-eight

"He's doing remarkably well. Nico is a strong young man." Doctor D'Angelo stood before them in his surgical scrubs. He briefed them all about Nico's surgery, explaining they were able to save his spleen. "We will keep him in *Terapia Intensiva* for now. We can let two of you in at a time for a quick visit. But please, keep it to a minimum. Right now, he just needs to rest."

"We'll follow your orders," Marco said firmly, glancing at the group. When he returned with Kate, he seemed calmer during their long wait. Kate and Ellie joined the other women in the corner, and they purposely seemed to keep the conversation light.

Georgie walked away from the group now and took heaving breaths. Margherita's voice came behind her. "We will take turns. Everyone can see him for a quick visit, and then I think we should all go home for the night. Georgie, I suggest you and Marco go in first. I'll go in next with Stefano."

Georgie turned and nodded, keeping her gaze averted. She walked silently down the hall with Marco toward the intensive care unit. Donning masks, they entered the unit and were directed to sliding glass doors on their right. Marco put a hand on her arm, and his concerned eyes searched hers. "Georgie, we need to recognize that he is going to look awful right now. But the doctor said he will improve each day."

Georgie stopped in her tracks. She had been so focused on seeing Nico she hadn't thought about how he would look. As her heart raced, fear filled her. Taking a step backward, she started to shake her head. She couldn't see him hurt. Nico was always so vibrant and alive. It would be devastating to see him any other way. Turning, she ran out the doors, but Marco was right on her heels.

"Georgie, *per favore*. Look at me!" Georgie leaned up against the wall with one hand. Her heart felt like it was galloping. Ripping her mask off, she stared at Marco, who lowered his own mask. His gaze swept intently over her.

"We need to go in," he said firmly.

"He's asleep. Even the doctor said so. He won't even know I'm there," Georgie argued. She felt weak for not being able to go in, but the thought of Nico laying there injured all because of her tore her heart in two.

Marco frowned. "*Si.* He's asleep. But he *will* wake up. And when he does, if he finds out you abandoned him again, neither of you will be able to come back from this. Three strikes and you're out, as they say in America."

"I'm English. We don't say that," Georgie reminded him. "Besides, I didn't abandon him!"

Marco's lips were in a tight line. He made a dismissive gesture. "That's what it felt like to him! I'm not going to play amateur psychologist. But Katie will tell you that we all suffer from our father's abandonment in different ways. The two times you broke up with Nico, he felt that pain. It may not be fair, and you may have good reasons. Katie has tried to get me to see your side," he said, smiling a little wryly. "But *per favore*, I'm asking you...I'm begging you to gather strength to go in there and be there for my brother right now. He was there for you when you needed him. And now he needs you. Nico told me you were one of the strongest people he's ever met."

"He told you that?" Georgie whispered. "I just told Meara I don't feel strong."

"*Si*, he told me you stood up to your father. You worked hard to get your pilot's license, despite no support. That even with him, you held your ground."

Georgie shook her head sadly. "I am so sorry, Marco. About everything. I don't care if you wanted to take over the land. It seems so meaningless now. Your company can have it."

"What are you talking about?" Marco asked sharply. "I do not understand."

"I heard you! Well, I heard Nico. I couldn't hear what you were saying, but you were having a discussion about Oro taking over my grandfather's land. And I became enraged. You see, I thought it was his legacy. Only, after giving it a lot of thought, and talking about it with my mother, I realize that it should have gone to Nico all along. He is the one who understands it and can cultivate it. *Nonno* knew that."

"Georgie," Marco said gently, a light coming into his eyes. "That's why you left?"

"That and, well, a few other things. But they are between me and Nico, if you don't mind. But yes, that was what made me angry enough to leave."

Marco shook his head in disbelief. "We weren't plotting a conspiracy against you! I just pointed out to Nico all the short-comings of keeping the farm in your names. Under the Oro umbrella, we can assist greatly. There are numerous regulations in Sicily regarding sustainability and water conservation. Nico has the agricultural expertise, but you must also have to work with government agronomists and legal advisors to ensure compliance with all regulations. Sicily is renowned for its agri-cultural heritage, and we already do this with our other properties and have gained compliance in all areas. No matter what you would still have a full say in what is done with the property."

Georgie stared at him with dismay. "Oh my God, what did I do? That all makes sense. I don't know how to apologize, Marco. Can you forgive me?"

Marco smiled a little for the first time. "It is not I who has to do the forgiving. It is my brother. And chances are he had something to do with your relationship troubles as well. Katie has taught me that takes two to make a mess of things. We Rinaldi's tend to act like steamrollers sometimes," he said and gave a small chuckle. "Destiny seems to continue to throw you and my brother into each other's path."

Stretching out a hand, he stared intently at her. "Now, how about we start the process and go in and see him? I'll be right there, holding your hand."

Georgie nodded and gave Marco a watery smile before tying her mask in place and grabbing his hand. She took several deep breaths before they walked through the unit, and Marco slid the door open. Nico was fast asleep, with tubes and drains attached to him. She glanced at the two monitors next to his bed, not understanding anything she was viewing. Marco slid a chair over to her, and she sat quickly, her legs like jelly. Leaning forward, she gently took Nico's uninjured hand—the other was wrapped with some kind of burn dressing. Staring at their clasped hands, tears swam in her eyes. There was no reflexive grip and no sign he was even aware she was there.

"His color is good," remarked Marco softly.

Georgie nodded, continuing to stroke Nico's warm hand.

She suddenly thought of something and turned to look at Marco. "Marco, why was Nico even at my *nonni*'s house?"

Marco's eyes crinkled a little, and he must have been smiling. "That is something he will have to tell you when he wakes up, Georgie."

twenty-nine

"You haven't been here all night, dear?" Margherita asked anxiously.

Georgie wiped her bleary eyes in surprise. Slowly, she stood and stretched her stiff back. Sometime in the middle of the night, the nurses slid a recliner in Nico's room and whispered to her it was okay if she stayed. That was a relief because Georgie had no intention of leaving. She spent the night curled up in the chair, occasionally drifting off for a brief amount of time. Mostly, she stayed focused on Nico's pale face while he slept, his beautiful long dark eyelashes hiding his usually bright eyes. Her mind acted like a carousel, swiftly advancing through images from their past.

It had been early morning, right when clarity had struck that while their love had been deep and profound when they were young, but they were only kids. Obviously, their love still burned deep, but they had to spend time to learn about the grown-up version of one another. For whatever reason, Nico rushed that process, and she had bolted. Deep down, Georgie acknowledged she played a role by sinking into herself, thinking it was the right thing to do to please Nico. Yet, her own independent streak just couldn't allow having another man telling her what to do. Nico needed to accept this Georgie, the one who flew a plane for a living and made her own decisions. Deep in her heart, she felt he would.

Throughout the night, she whispered her love to him, gently stroking his hand as she tried to explain everything. At one point, she thought he smiled a little. Perhaps it was a grimace. Still hoping he heard her, she finally felt at peace. "I'm not leaving you again," she promised.

Glancing at Margherita now, she smiled a little. "I think he's better. His color has improved. Some alarms went off in the middle of the night, but the nurses reassured me that was to be expected. His oxygen level is much better." At Margherita's raised eyebrows, Georgie flushed. "I asked the nurses a lot of questions last night about all of it. I couldn't stare at all those numbers without knowing what they signified. I'm used to looking at numbers in the cockpit, if you see what I mean."

Margherita walked over and gently put her arms around Georgie. "*Grazie*," she whispered. Pulling away, she stared at her son. "He does look better. Now we just need him to wake up."

"They have been keeping him sedated for a reason," Alec said as he entered the room. "They are pulling back a little on his medication gradually, and he should come around soon. The doctors will be around to tend to him in a few minutes. Perhaps it's a good time to get some fresh air."

"But I want to be here when he wakes!" Georgie argued.

Alec smiled gently. "Let's allow the medical staff to care for him, and when they are finished, I'll call for you."

Margherita kissed Nico gently on the forehead and turned to leave. Georgie followed suit, brushing his beautiful hair to the side. "I'll be back. I'm not leaving," she reiterated in his ear.

～

"HE'S AWAKE AND GROGGY, but he wants to see Georgie," Alec said, glancing at the crowded waiting area. "Sorry, everyone, but he said Georgie only."

"Of course," Margherita said, giving Georgie a hug. "Tell him we are all here."

Georgie felt like her heart was beating out of her chest as she walked down the long hallway. Last night, it seemed so easy to spill all her thoughts and feelings to him. Now that he was awake, she was terrified of what he would say and do. Was he going to tell her to go away? Was he going to say his love had died? Her heart couldn't bear it. No matter what he said, she was staying. Nothing was going to change her mind.

Sliding the glass door open, she gently closed it behind her and stared at Nico over her mask. His eyes were closed, and she gently perched on the edge of the chair next to him. That seemed to startle him, and his dark eyes blinked open. "George," he said, his voice raspy. "You're here."

Georgie nodded and wordlessly picked up his uninjured hand to hold it. This time, he gripped back, and her eyes filled with tears of relief. "I'm here to stay," she choked.

"Pull down your mask, George. I need to see your face."

She glanced out of the door to see if any nurses were around. "They want us to wear them so you don't catch any germs."

Nico swore in Italian. "I need to see your face."

She obeyed his request, and he studied her intently. Finally, he whispered, "How long are you staying?"

"Forever."

He blinked, and she saw tears and sadness in his eyes. "I'm not sure I believe you."

She gave him a small smile. "I understand. We have so much to talk about. But I'm here, Nico, if you'll have me. And I'll spend my whole life proving to you that I will never leave."

"I heard you last night."

"You did?"

He smiled a little. "I thought it was a dream. I heard you talking. I couldn't really make out what you were saying, but I knew you were here. I tried to send you a signal and tried to smile to let you know I was okay. But I couldn't open my eyes. I was hoping when I woke up it wasn't a dream. When Alec told me you were here I...well, I didn't know what to think."

"It isn't a dream," she said, tightening her hold.

His eyes were still filled with doubt, and it made her heart ache. "George, can you do me a favor then?"

"Anything," she whispered.

"Kiss me."

She grinned, and her heart burst in relief. Bending over, she gave him a gentle kiss, their lips barely touching.

"It's definitely not a dream," he said and closed his eyes.

<h1 style="text-align:center">thirty</h1>

Georgie purposely slowed her steps, realizing the last thing she needed to do was run and trip. Today was too important. After weeks of surgeries, Nico was finally able to come home! His internal injuries had healed, and the burns on his hand were drastically improved. After metal plates and screws had been surgically placed in his leg, he now wore a complicated state-of-the-art splint. The doctors warned Nico he would need to take it very easy for several weeks, and Georgie was going to ensure he did so.

During his stay in the hospital, they had mutually agreed to put their relationship on hold while he cleared the next hurdles. His family visited often, but also seemed to be intent on giving them privacy. Sometimes, Georgie secretly wished they would stay, for Nico was a tough patient, restless and impatient to improve. Georgie reassured Nico's family that she would remain and was touched by their stated trust.

To occupy his mind, she brought him a chessboard and taught him to play. He roughly pushed it aside after a day. The next day she brought a cribbage board, which didn't go over any better. A deck of cards was next, and that seemed a little more palatable. They played every game they knew until he was tired of that, too. Monopoly was next, and that seemed to cheer him up a little. Often, she found herself losing, as Nico bought every piece of real estate and was a ruthless landlord. Watching his restlessness, she knew she would have her work cut out for her at the villa.

While Nico rested in the afternoons, Georgie went shopping for a new wardrobe and last night, she packed it up in her hotel room. Marco firmly insisted on having a driver take them to Taormina, and the car was now waiting outside as Georgie went to collect Nico.

She was shocked when her father's name appeared on her phone. She almost let it go to voicemail, but decided to answer it to get it over with. While she had been in communication with her mother about Nico, she had not given her father a thought.

"Georgina, your mother told me you are still in Sicily," he stated.

"Hello, Dad. And yes, I am. Once Nico is well, the two of us are going to plan our future together. Please don't try to talk me out of it!"

"I wasn't going to dissuade you, Georgina," her father said quietly. "Niccolo is deeply in love with you. I realize that now. And I also understand how he has made quite a name for himself, too. You should be proud of him."

Georgie sat down in a hallway chair, stunned. Eventually, her father chuckled. "I bet you never thought I would say that."

"You are correct. Do you want to tell me what changed your mind? His family's wealth?" she asked suspiciously.

"Not at all. I knew about his family's wealth—hard not to, really. His brother is in the news nearly every day. But once we sat down and talked, I was impressed by his commitment to his field."

"What do you mean, sat down?" Georgie exploded.

"He didn't tell you? He came to Paris to see me several weeks ago."

Georgie frowned. "He hasn't said a word. But we agreed to not talk about our relationship for the time being. Right now, his focus must be on healing."

"I admit, I was surprised. But I agreed to meet with him, and we talked for some time. Georgina, I am not the ogre you make me out to be. I only want what is best for you."

"I am sorry I have disappointed you," Georgie said. "I should never have let everything get as out of control as it did with my wedding."

"Yes, your near wedding cost me a fair bit, not to mention the personal embarrassment. But your mother's made it clear that, in the end, it was mostly my fault. I pushed you into it. Over the years, I know I have been far more rigid than I should have been in my thinking."

"You have talked to Mum?"

"Yes, she is here with me now. We are working at reconciling."

"She never said a word!"

He laughed again, almost an unfamiliar sound to Georgie. "We did not want to discuss it with you unless we made some decisions. Last night, we agreed to make our marriage a priority."

Georgie smiled a little. "I am happy for you both."

"Your mother's been trying to change me back to the man she married. I'm not quite there yet, Georgina. I'm still stubborn and set in my ways at times. But I'm trying," he said.

She smiled. "I am pleased to hear that, Daddy. Maybe soon I can fly over and see you."

The silence almost made her laugh. He was still struggling. Finally, he spoke. "That would be nice, Georgina."

"Daddy, if we are going to move forward, let's start with the first big step."

"And that is?"

"Call me Georgie," she said cheerfully.

"I AM SO SORRY!" Georgie said urgently, trying not to focus on Nico's dark look, as she picked up the weight she had just dropped near his foot. In the past few days, she felt like she couldn't do anything right. They had been in Taormina for a week, and it had been a busy one. A physical therapist came daily, leading him through breathing exercises to build his lungs up after the exposure to smoke. Nico was also shown which light weights in his home gym to use and was slowly beginning to strengthen his tired muscles. Disappointed in his progress, he was making life difficult for everyone in the near vicinity.

"I swear, George, you're trying to kill me!"

She bit back a nervous giggle. "I'm not. I'm just clumsy. You know that."

"I don't know if it was you being clumsy or if you wanted to dump that water on me earlier."

She smiled. "Well, you needed some cooling off after the doctor left. You weren't very nice to her, Nico. She was trying to be encouraging about how well you are doing."

Nico swore in Italian before taking a deep breath and continuing in English. "Maybe she thinks so! She's not trapped in this stupid splint! I need to get on with my life! I can't even walk in my own garden, let alone take care of my plants!"

Georgie tried not to roll her eyes. She needed more patience. "I know you've been through a lot, but you've still got a way to go, Nico. You need to do your exercises. When you get stronger, you can do all that!"

"Why are you even here?" he growled. "What about your job? Don't you have someplace to fly to?"

She frowned. "I am on leave. I told you that!"

He shifted uncomfortably on his workout bench. "You don't have to stay. I am fine. I have nurses and physical therapists to take care of me."

Georgie tried not to be hurt. They had not spoken a word about their relationship, and there was a lot of ground to cover when he got well.

"Nico, I want to be here."

"Did it ever occur to you that I don't want you here?"

It was like he'd struck her. His gaze softened. He had seen the hurt in her eyes. "Then I'll leave," she said softly.

As she went to walk past him, he reached out and grabbed her hand. "George, please don't go," he rasped. "Don't leave."

"I was just going to go for a swim," she said gently. "Not leave as in pack up and go. Listen, you are the worst patient in the world. I know we said we would wait to talk, and I promise I won't leave unless you want me to afterwards."

He nodded and slowly let go of her hand. A bell chimed in the distance.

"Your physical therapist is here," she commented. "Time to work."

NICO SAT in the chair again, sweat beading his brow. The physical therapist had put him through the paces, and he cooperated without complaining. Georgie was right that he wouldn't get stronger without putting forth the work. The last several weeks had been physically painful, but the time with Georgie was also frustrating because Georgie refused to talk about their future until he healed.

It was understandable that she was here. Remorse did that to a person. When it occurred to him in the hospital she was there because she felt guilty, his anger rose. Now she undoubtedly pitied him. He was a terrible patient, but mostly it was because of his misery that when he was finally healed, she would take off again. Their relationship wouldn't survive if it was based on her feeling responsible for his injuries. The only acceptable reason for her to be with him would be because she couldn't live without him. Georgie's fierce independence defied that thought. She didn't need anyone.

Selling the land to her had been the right thing to do. It sent a clear message that it wasn't as important to him as she was. Still, she had not mentioned it once. He worried it was all withering away now that no one was caring for it. Many times, he opened his mouth to ask her about it and then decided not to. It was killing him, thinking of that valuable and wonderful land decaying because of neglect.

He also longed to discover how much of her grandparents' house had burned or if it had spread to the property. No one told him in the hospital, and Marco was noncommittal at best. When the fire broke out, Nico had been at the property. He had smelled the pungent odor first and then saw the smoke billow out from an upstairs window. After calling the fire brigade, he ran in and grabbed the boxes of photos and memorabilia that he had seen on the table. Then he went back to the porch for *Nonno's* rocking chair. The third time he ran inside the house for one last memento and that was when part of the beam must have fallen on him. He blacked out immediately. All he knew was that the firefighters had rescued him, and he was flown by helicopter to Palermo.

Nico took a drink of the water the physical therapist had left for him. There were so many questions, and he needed answers. He and Georgie needed to settle things. It wasn't a nurse he needed. It was her! And if she was there to salve her own feelings of shame, then she needed to leave.

Angrily, he slammed down the glass, and water slopped over on the table. It was time! Tonight, they would talk.

thirty-one

"Why did you want to eat out here?" Georgie asked, looking around at the many candles lining the poolside and the torches around the patio. "It's easier for you to just eat in the dining room then have to walk all the way out here."

For the first time that day, Nico grinned. "I thought it was time I left the house. Even if it's only to the garden. The physical therapist told me I needed to walk more, so here I am."

Georgie nodded and took another bite. She had been oddly touched to find the server bringing out all her favorite foods. Fried eggplant, fresh artichokes stuffed with breadcrumbs and sharp parmesan cheese, and *arancini* filled with rice and prosciutto were set before them. Angelina's special stuffed *rigatoni* was next. While she should be enjoying it, she couldn't stop feeling uneasy. Glancing at Nico, she saw he was sitting back in his comfortable chair, watching her intently. He had barely touched his dinner. She indicated it. "Are you not hungry?"

"I had a late *aperitivo*."

Georgie frowned. Was that a dig? She had purposely avoided going down to have an *aperitivo* with him earlier. It had seemed a good idea to give him space after his earlier eruption.

"We need to talk, Georgie," he said quietly.

Her heart sunk. He was about to send her home. She had seen the defeated look in his eyes earlier. When he had first woken up in the hospital, she thought she had seen the glimmer of hope in his eyes. As time passed, he had become increasingly disgruntled. At first, she put it down to his injuries and impatience at healing. But as time wore on, she sensed his mood shift toward her. It was almost as if he was getting angrier with her as the days wore on.

Finally, lifting her gaze to his steady one, she put down her fork with a clang. "Alright. Talk."

His eyes widened, almost as if he hadn't expected her to acquiesce so easily. "I know we agreed in the hospital that we would put the subject of us on hold, but it is not working for me. I need to know where you stand. Where we stand."

"I told you I am here for you."

"For how long?" he bit out, running his hand through his hair. "Georgie, what happened to us? Why did you leave after one misunderstanding? I thought...well, I thought we had come farther than that."

Suddenly, her own anger began to bubble up. She had thrust it down deep when she found out he had been hurt. "Why am I continually reminded about my leaving, yet you are somehow blameless?"

"What exactly did I do?" he asked icily.

"Everything!" Standing up, she paced. "I could barely catch my breath. After I broke my arm, it was like you were on a mission to impress me. Fancy dinners, spendy surprises around every turn! Gigantic diamonds. I know, I know. What girl wouldn't want that, right?"

Her tone softened as she saw the muscle twitching in his jaw. "It was all lovely. But it wasn't me. It wasn't you either. It was like you were putting on a show for me. Did you think I needed all that to be with you? Then you suddenly asked me to marry you…only after that, you didn't want to talk about our future. It almost felt like we were in a play, and you were the lead. I was just in the chorus. But I went along with it. Do you know why?"

He gave a subtle shake of his head.

"Because I love you, you idiot. I've always loved you. But every day, I saw a little less of myself. I started to shrink inside. It reminded me of how I felt trying to please my father."

"Do not compare me to him!" Nico said angrily.

Georgie drew out the chair next to Nico and sat gazing at him. "In many ways, you are alike. Stubborn, like to have your own way…" She smiled gently. "And you both love me."

At his silence, she continued. "Which brings me to my next point. Why did you visit him?"

"I wanted his approval."

Georgie stared at him, startled. "But we had broken off."

Nico smiled sadly. "It didn't matter that we weren't together. I went to him for his approval, and then the funniest thing happened. When I walked into the restaurant where we agreed to meet, I looked at him, and he didn't seem as powerful anymore. He was just a man. He looked older and sad, I guess. And I realized he was a man who cared deeply for his daughter's welfare. Suddenly it didn't seem to matter anymore what he thought of me."

"You impressed him."

"I no longer set out to. That's the funniest thing. I guess I'm just likeable." He suddenly grinned disarmingly, his dimples showing for the first time in weeks.

Georgie put her hand over his. "I think so, too. Even loveable."

"I am sorry, Georgie. Thinking back now, I was trying desperately to give you what I thought you wanted. I twisted you and your father up and somehow thought you desired all the extravagance. Flashing the wealth usually works with the ladies," he teased.

She raised an eyebrow. "Oh, it does, does it? Well, not with this lady. It just wasn't you. It wasn't us. And then the proposal…"

"A little public, wasn't it?"

Georgie could only nod, averting her gaze.

"I guess there was a part of me that was competing with your past."

She looked at him, raising her eyebrows, and he continued. "I was desperate to put a ring on your finger. Somehow, I thought that would make you want to stay."

"I already wanted to stay," Georgie told him quietly. "But I wanted to be a partner in every sense of the word. When we went back to Nizza and you were so dismissive of me, it seemed like I wasn't even allowed to be involved with decisions regarding the land."

His fingers stroked her palm, sending tingles up her spine. "I'm sorry about that, too. I meant what I said at the time. I'm just not used to anyone caring about it. I wasn't trying to steal the property from you. I was trying to protect *Nonno*'s land—"

"I know! Marco explained," she interrupted. "He didn't have to, though," she added quickly. "When I thought it through, I knew there had to be another explanation. Only you were acting so different and secretive. I didn't know about you flying everyone in for the *festa*. I'm sorry for everything, Nico, and I never thanked you."

Leaning forward, he gave her the briefest of kisses. "Thanks are unnecessary. I only wanted you to be happy. What if we start over again?"

"We tried that before. Somehow we can't get this right."

He chuckled. "What if we take this slower and get to know each other as adults?"

"Did you hear what I said in the hospital?" she asked incredulously.

"No. I was only aware you were there. I told you I thought it was a dream."

Grinning at him, she squeezed his hand. "I said the same thing. I wanted time together. But this time around, authentic and no pretending."

Glancing down at their clasped hands, she frowned.

"What's the matter, Georgie?"

"Why were you so angry at me for the last few weeks?"

He looked chagrined. "When I first saw you in the hospital, I thought you had come because you loved me. My heart was about to burst. But then I convinced myself you were there because you felt guilty."

"Oh, Nico, how could you think that?"

"Well, I did risk my life for some things that meant a lot to you," he said in a wheedling tone.

"Yes, about that. How could you? Nothing means more to me than you!"

He smiled gently. "*Grazie, cara.* But I couldn't bear watching the fire without trying. It moved faster than I thought," he said with a grimace. "I retrieved a few boxes and *Nonno's* chair from the porch. Then I ran back in."

"For what?"

Reaching into his shirt pocket, he brought out a small charred wooden frame she had been holding on the porch for what seemed like an eternity ago. "Us," he said huskily.

thirty-two

"I could have driven," Nico grumbled as Georgie steered his Jeep up the hill in Nizza di Sicilia.

"Your splint has been off for two days."

Nico leaned over and put a hand on her jean-clad thigh. "Thanks for taking care of me, George," he said softly. Glancing at his now tender eyes, she almost ran off the road.

"Behave yourself, Niccolo," she mocked. "Or I'm going to drive us into a ditch. You drive on the wrong side of the road in this country!"

"I am sure you can handle it," he remarked. "You are remarkably skilled. You have driven me all over these last few weeks."

"Does that mean you're going to fly with me?"

He laughed. "Let's not get ahead of ourselves. But I just might."

Georgie smiled. It had been a lovely month. Once Nico transitioned to a lighter brace, they had been able to go on more outings. But her favorite thing to do had been to stay home in his quiet villa. They dismissed the staff except for his visiting physical therapist. They cooked together and swam—well, she swam while he did small exercises while sitting in the shallow end. He said he didn't mind if it meant watching her glide in the clear blue pool in her red bikini.

Their conversations were frank and honest, and Georgie felt their level of closeness only deepen. The only thing lacking was their physical intimacy. Though Nico kissed her with a frustrated passion, he left her at her own bedroom door each night. Grudgingly, she slept alone. This getting to know each other before resuming anything physical was getting old. Yet at the same time, Georgie felt a sense of peace about their time together.

Now she glanced at Nico. He was looking out the window, the wind ruffling his thick black hair. Suddenly, he looked tense.

"Nico, you haven't asked the whole time I've been with you about the farm or the lemon grove."

He still didn't look at her. "It's yours, George. I want to prove to you that I understand that."

"It's not really mine," she teased. "I never gave you your one Euro. Nor did I sign the papers. So, the deal never went through. Besides, you know I don't know what I'm doing."

He glanced over at her, but she couldn't see his eyes behind his sunglasses. When he spoke, it was with conviction. "I trust you to do the right thing."

Georgie grinned as they pulled up to the farm, and she set the parking brake. "That's the first time you've told me that, Nico. It feels wonderful," she said quietly.

He was still staring at her, and she laughed. "Go ahead and look!"

He took off his glasses and turned to view the house. Getting slowly out of the Jeep, his head swiveled. "It's been completely rebuilt!"

Laughing, she went over and grabbed his hand. "When you were in the hospital, I told Marco to do what he had to do. I signed over the land to Oro, and he put Giovanni in charge of managing the operation of the entire farm as well. Everything has been taken care of."

"Why didn't you tell me?"

"I wanted you to trust me. And I wanted to surprise you."

He glanced up at the house, which had dramatically increased in size. "The house is a little more…"

"Stately?"

He laughed. "Yes, I guess you could call it that."

"Let's be honest, Nico. It always felt like home to me, but it definitely needed modernizing. The Fire Inspector said the fire started in the attic and it was probably due to old wires. In the end, I realized without my grandparents, it wasn't a home anymore. It needs people. So I asked Giovanni if he'd like to move his family into one wing of it."

"But, George…"

"Oh, we'll still visit," she said with a smile. "But I still want to ensure it is lived in and loved. *Nonno* would want it that way."

They stood looking at the hectares of lemon trees before them. "Nico, I asked Marco, and he wouldn't tell me. Why were you even here the day the house caught on fire? You already offered to sell me the land by that time."

He grinned down at her before kissing her gently. Taking her shoulders, he turned her around to face down the hill to the north of the trees. "I was overseeing that."

She squinted down the hill. "A landing strip? You built me a landing strip?"

"Well, not me personally. But, yes, I had it built."

She turned and threw her arms around him. In one simple act, he had shown her how much he believed in her. "Thank you, Nico."

"*Prego*," he acknowledged softly.

"You are really okay with me still flying?"

He smiled a little. "Will I worry? Yes, George. But I support your passion just as you support mine. I'll dig in the earth while you take to the skies. Just always come home to me," he whispered before his lips descended on hers.

thirty-three

"You are sure you are feeling okay? You are still so pale!" Georgie exclaimed. She had landed her sleek, new plane on the landing strip that Nico built in Nizza. It had been months since they were back at the farm together. Despite insisting he believed in Giovanni, Nico had visited a few times on his own to check in. It made her smile, thinking how Nico was so like her grandfather in that way. Though he could delegate the work, he had to see for himself the land was thriving.

She had been shocked when he suggested she fly them both to Sicily. At first, she thought he was calm, but as they flew, he seemed to get increasingly nervous.

"I'm fine!" he reassured her. "Honestly, George, you are an expert pilot. I didn't once fear for my life."

"Well, that's the goal," she joked. "Nico, I love my new plane," she said softly. He had surprised her with it a few weeks prior. Though she would still fly the medical transport planes, it was nice to have a smaller, state-of-the-art one for getaways like this.

"I didn't think the runway here could quite handle a jet," he said with a laugh. He grabbed her hand, and they headed over to his Jeep.

"Nico, how do things just magically appear for you?"

He grinned. "Very little magic involved, George. I asked Giovanni to bring it down."

"But we can just walk up the hill to the farm."

"We aren't going to the farm," he explained, helping her into the Jeep.

She waited for him to get into the driver's seat. "Where are we going?"

"Our lemon grove. Where we started," he said, giving her a small smile.

Georgie looked out the window as they drove past the neat rows of lemon trees. Taking a breath, she smelled the sweet smell of her beloved Sicily. It felt great to be back. She had resumed flying while Nico was busy with a series of lectures on regenerative farming. The symposium in Amsterdam in which he was a guest speaker was packed, and Georgie had surprised him, slipping in the back of one. She was bursting with pride. "It was like being with a rock star. A very nerdy rock star," she told him later, watching the throngs of people trying to speak with him.

They spent as much time together as possible, and she even managed to coax him to London, where she had taken him on days of sightseeing. While he enjoyed the traditional sights of Buckingham Palace and the Tower of London, he looked more at home at the farmer's market on Notting Hill. This time, when he met her friends, he looked comfortable and confident.

"He's so dishy. Does he have a single brother?" Mary whispered. "I'm begging you!"

Georgie had only giggled and went over to link her arm through his. He was all hers. They hadn't talked about their future, but she was fine with that. Just as long as he continued to look at her with love in his eyes. It made her heart sing.

She jumped out of the Jeep at the lemon grove. "We haven't been here since the *festa*," she remarked.

"Since I kissed you for the first time."

She grabbed his hand and smiled at him as they walked toward the grove, ducking between the trees. "Which first time?" she said with a laugh. "You kissed me when I was sixteen here, too."

They strolled through the grove, stopping to admire the trees. "Even I can tell it looks so much better," Georgie said, smiling up at him. "Thank you, Nico."

He shrugged. "It's all Giovanni. I just make sure everyone has what they need."

As they walked toward the stone bench, she squinted. "Nico, there's something on our bench! Is that writing?"

She dropped his hand and ran toward it. Sure enough, there was an engraving on the bench.

"Per sempre il nostro amore fiorirà."

"Forever our love will bloom," she translated softly, turning to Nico. She looked down. He was bent on one knee.

"Oh, Nico," she whispered.

He smiled gently up at her. Grabbing her left hand, he slowly maneuvered the promise ring off her finger, putting it on her right hand. He then took another ring and put it on her ring finger. She blinked at it, her eyes widening. It was a replica of her small promise ring, but this one had a thicker rose gold band with a larger garnet and sapphire.

"Georgie, we met in this very grove. We fell in love in this grove. And though it took us a long time to get back here, our love is now stronger. It is now thriving and as nourished as these trees. We made a promise a long time ago. And now I am asking you to accept another vow. Will you share my life? We are from two worlds, yet our paths intersect where it is important. Today I ask for your heart so we can begin our next chapter of this fascinating story we have spun together."

Tears slid down her cheeks. Slowly, she pulled Nico to his feet. Putting a hand on either side of his face, she kissed him slowly. "I promise," she said huskily.

thirty-four

"You look beautiful, darling."

Georgie smiled at her mother and then looked over at her father. He looked almost jovial today. "You both look spectacular. Thank you for accepting this wedding. I know it is a little unconventional."

Georgie wanted to laugh out loud and remember her parents' expression when they heard she and Nico would be wed in a lemon grove. Her mother probably imagined the previous *festa*, which had been lively, but rustic.

"Georgina...uh Georgie, we have enjoyed getting to know Nico's family," her father remarked. "And anywhere you decide to get married is fine by us. Or so your mother has convinced me," he added with a laugh.

Georgie could only grin happily. Her parents had flown in and spent several days with Nico's family at their estate. While at first they had been overwhelmed by the chaos and constant laughter, eventually they relaxed, to Georgie's amazement and pride. She whispered to her mother that she had never seen her father so approachable.

Her mother smiled. "It should have happened years ago. He

is back to being the man I fell in love with. We both lost our way for a time, but we found each other again."

"Just like me and Nico," Georgie remarked.

She flew her parents down to the farm and, after their initial uneasiness, they relaxed enough to tell her she seemed to know what she was doing. A high compliment, she said with a laugh. Next, she turned them over to Giovanni, who was waiting to welcome them into the newly remodeled home. Georgie and her mother exchanged discreet glances, knowing that it was vastly improved. Marco had extended the home by almost 6,000 feet, adding bedrooms and modern appliances. Remarkably, her grandmother's old ravioli table had survived the fire, and it now stood in the large farmhouse kitchen. Even though it looked a little out of place with the Italian tile and stainless-steel appliances, Georgie still loved it. She wasn't surprised when her father proclaimed the house "lovely."

From the moment they got engaged again, Nico's family had been incredibly kind and loving. "Told you so," Meara nudged her. "Nico is always going to love you."

Georgie smiled, but it took a lot more than love to get them where they were today. It took trust, respect and understanding of how far they had come.

The family worked nonstop to help create the wedding of their dreams in a little over a month. Now that they had decided, they didn't want to wait. Georgie oversaw all the details with Margherita. A large white tent was erected in the empty space beyond the lemon grove. Little fairy lights were everywhere, including the numerous Italian pots that contained flowers and plants. The more greenery the better, Georgie told Margherita. "Nico needs to feel like he's at home with his plants!"

Georgie was whisked away to Milan with all the women, Francesca leading the charge. They were severely disappointed at Georgie's quick decision making. "You can't choose the first dress you try on!" Francesca scolded her. Georgie only laughed and submitted to several more dresses before going back to slip on the simple designer sheath. It had a plunging V-neck in front and back, both embroidered with pearls. The dress was her choice this time. She wore her hair down, pearl clips pinning it up at the crown.

Now waiting to walk down the makeshift aisle with both of her parents at her side, she laughed a little watching Frankie tottering as ring bearer. Alec and Meara's daughter, Valentina, strong-armed him, keeping him on a steady path. Mary was next, and then Georgie began to walk, and Nico's slow grin spread across his face. Images of a boy grinning at her like that flashed before her eyes before the adult Nico's face came back into view. They had been through so much. Tonight they would begin their forever lives together.

"HAVE I told you how breathtaking you look?" Nico whispered in her ear, sending shivers down her spine. *"Sei così bella."*

Georgie smiled up at him as they danced. "Only about a dozen times. But feel free to keep on."

He pulled her tighter. "Let's sneak away."

"We can't! It's our wedding reception," Georgie admonished, pushing at his shoulder. He pulled away to grin at her before hugging her.

"It's our wedding night as well, *cara,*" Nico reminded her quietly. "I wish you would have agreed to go somewhere besides my villa. We could be on Marco's yacht. Sail to Sardinia or Greece even."

"We'll do that later," she told him. "Just me and you in Taormina. That's all I want." Her heart raced at the thought.

She looked down at the rose gold wedding band on her finger, and tears rose in her eyes. "Nico, how did you get *Nonna's* wedding band?"

He hugged her tighter. "*Nonno* gave it to me after she passed, *amore mio.*"

"But what if we hadn't gotten together?"

Nico pulled back, his beautiful eyes resting on her face. "Fate was always going to pull us together, George."

Georgie snuggled into his arms, looking over his shoulder at their guests, composed of family, friends and the community of Nizza, who had been honored to be invited. Everyone was obviously enjoying themselves. Speeches were made, food was in abundance, and the tables looked exquisite. She grinned at her parent's expressions when they saw the sparkling China and silver, the massive centerpieces dotting the tables. It looked just as wonderful, if not better, than any venue they had been to in London. Not to mention, each course of the dinner had been a delicious culinary experience. Stefano oversaw the catering team, and Teresa had explained how everything was held to his high standards.

Earlier, they had cut their four-tier cake, decorated by Ellie, who insisted it was now a family tradition. Everyone had been involved in one way or another. Georgie truly was a part of another family now. Once an only child, she now relished the thought of having so many brothers and sisters.

"Let's just sneak out for just a minute," Nico whispered again in her ear. "They won't even know we're gone. We'll come back soon; I promise."

"You can kiss me here," she teased.

He stared at her, his gaze burning with heated passion. "Not like I want to."

Letting him lead her out of the tent discreetly, Georgie felt her heart racing. Turning at a sharp voice, she saw Francesca on the phone, speaking angrily in rapid Italian. Georgie stopped for a moment, concerned for her new friend. "I won't come home," Francesca said defiantly. "I have a new life now."

Nico glanced back at her and shrugged as if to say it was not their business. Georgie remained for a moment before recognizing he was probably right. She followed him up the stone path to their lemon grove.

Turning abruptly, he thrust his hands in her hair, hauling her close. Kissing her passionately, he simply took all the breath from her body. It was a long time later before he finally pulled away. She put a hand up to her disheveled hair and knew her lips were probably swollen from his kisses.

"Everyone is going to know what we've been doing," she teased, straightening her dress.

"Don't care," he said, leaning in to resume kissing her. "You are finally my wife."

"I loved your vows," she said tremendously. "I didn't know you were going to say that."

He smiled gently at her. *"Per sempre il nostro amore fiorirà."*

She smiled tremulously. "Just like our bench says."

"Forever my love. Fate has her wish.

upcoming books

Looking for your next sweet romance from Italy?

Check out the next in the series—
Francesca's story:
My Valentine in Verona

E-Book Available Now!
Paperbacks available at Amazon or your favorite bookstore

Dear Reader:

Thank you for traveling to my beloved Sicily to experience this magical island. With my ancestors coming from Sicily, it was my honor to trace their footsteps alongside my brother Edward. It was Edward who arranged for a special tour of Nizza di Sicilia where we were warmly greeted by Mayor Piero Briguglio, and Giovanni Caminiti Interdonato – President of Consorzio Limone Interdonato Messina IGP. Standing in a 15th Century lemon grove in the hills of this beautiful coastal town can certainly spark creativity!

Thank you also to my sister-in-law Debbie (proofreader extraordinaire), who accompanied us on this wild journey, bringing her humor and sense of adventure. To my husband, Scott, thank you for packing up enthusiastically— always supporting my wild ideas. Thank you to my idea generator and dear friend, Mary.

If you want more...there is! Tour through more regions of Italy in this series: *From Italy with Love*. We'll travel all over, but we'll always swing by the Amalfi Coast to say hi to the family.

Grab some delicious pasta or a gelato and enjoy more from Italia! Remember to sign up for my newsletter at Tessrini.com/news-letter to read a bonus chapter from *My Secret Positano*.

Cin Cin!
XO, Tess

Tess Rini has spent her professional life focused on non-fiction writing, from her journalism degree to her editing and writing magazine articles and content for local government. She has published one non-fiction book under a different name.

Tess was raised on a self-induced steady diet of Harlequin romances and so it was inevitable that she should try her hand at romance writing. The idea took off when she combined her love of Italy with her love for romance novels.

When not writing, she can be found relaxing in her Oregon home, traveling or cooking Italian cuisine (her specialty!) for her husband, four daughters and son-in-law. Keeping her company while writing or watching Hallmark movies is her adorable, but anxious, golden retriever.

Sign up for her newsletter at Tessrini.com/newsletter to read a bonus chapter from My Secret Positano and stay up on all the latest Italy news.

Website: tessrini.com
Or follow her on social
Facebook @tessriniauthor
Instagram @tessrininauthor

www.ingramcontent.com/pod-product-compliance
Lightning Source LLC
Chambersburg PA
CBHW061522310726
48972CB00008B/2295